A MERRY BRAMBLEWICK CHRISTMAS

Recovering from a break-up, Izzy is throwing herself into the primary school Christmas play — it's a huge project, even with fellow teacher and volunteer assistant Ash by her side. As Christmas draws nearer and the snow begins to fall, Izzy and Ash develop a warm and growing attraction. But Izzy's best friend Anna has been acting coldly towards her since she revealed the reason her last relationship ended. With Anna judging her so harshly, dare Izzy tell Ash the truth about herself and risk everything they have built so far?

SHARON BOOTH

A MERRY BRAMBLEWICK CHRISTMAS

Complete and Unabridged

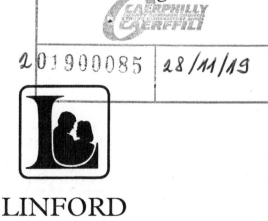

LINFORD
Leicester

First published in Great Britain in 2018

First Linford Edition
published 2019

A catalogue record for this book is available
from the British Library.

ISBN 978–1–4448–4325–5

Published by
F. A. Thorpe (Publishing)
Anstey, Leicestershire

Set by Words & Graphics Ltd.
Anstey, Leicestershire
Printed and bound in Great Britain by
T. J. International Ltd., Padstow, Cornwall

This book is printed on acid-free paper

1

Izzy leaned back in the armchair and closed her eyes. It was probably a mistake, she thought, aware that she was struggling to stay awake. She'd had a busy day and sitting here in the living room of Chestnut House, with the wood burner throwing out soothing heat and Michael Bublé's voice in the background to lull her to sleep, it would be all too easy to forget about everything and drift off into blissful unconsciousness.

'Gracie's asleep.'

Anna's voice penetrated the cosy fog that was beginning to cloud Izzy's brain, and she opened her eyes reluctantly, yawning as she did so.

'Sorry, did I wake you?' Anna sounded amused, as well she might. After all, if anyone had the right to be tired it was her, since she'd spent the day helping out at their friend Nell's cottage, The

Ducklings, along with everyone else, despite being over seven months pregnant.

'No, course not. I was just resting my eyes.' Izzy reached for her mug of coffee and took a sip, hoping the caffeine would give her some energy. 'What were you saying?'

'I said Gracie's asleep,' Anna repeated, landing on the sofa with a relieved sigh. 'I'm so glad. I thought she was too hyped up and she'd be awake all night, but it seems hard physical labour has done the trick. Good idea of Nell's to get her to help out with the house move, I must say.'

'Nell's not daft,' Izzy pointed out. 'She's had seven of us helping Riley move in to-day, including Gracie and Sam, and all it cost her was a few coffees and some pastries.' Gracie was Anna's ten-year-old stepdaughter, who tolerated, rather than liked, Sam, the seven-year-old son of their friend, Rachel. The two children had been shamelessly bribed by Nell to help out for the whole day and had thrown themselves into the job with surprising enthusiasm.

'Nice pastries, though,' Anna said. She lifted her legs onto the sofa and groaned. 'Look at my ankles! I look like a Cabbage Patch doll.'

Izzy giggled. 'Yeah, you do a bit. It's all right, though, isn't it? I mean, it doesn't mean anything's wrong?'

'Connor says everything's fine. He's obsessed with my blood pressure but it's always normal. I just seem to have developed fat ankles. I really hope they deflate after this baby arrives.'

'If not, you'll have to wear moon boots all the time,' Izzy suggested helpfully, earning a sarcastic smile from Anna. 'Are you feeling okay, anyway? You probably shouldn't have been helping out with the move, you know. You've only got a few weeks to go and you should be taking it easy.'

'So everyone keeps telling me,' Anna said, sounding gloomy. 'To be honest, I'm amazed Connor let me go. He's so flipping protective! I'm bored stiff now I'm on maternity leave.'

Izzy spluttered with laughter. 'You

left work on *Friday*! It's only been two days. Honestly, Anna, you're going to have to get used to it. Anyway, make the most of it because once Junior arrives you won't have a minute's peace.'

'I know.' Anna smiled and patted her swollen stomach gently. 'He doesn't give me much peace now, to be honest. Always rolling around and kicking me. Think he's going to be a professional footballer.'

'You're sure it's a boy?'

'No, not at all. One day I call it *he* and the next day it's *she*. I have no idea and no preference.'

'Does Connor mind?'

'Connor just wants a healthy baby,' Anna said.

'And Gracie?'

'She's hoping for a puppy.'

They burst out laughing.

'Think she's going to be a bit disappointed then,' Izzy said. 'Although, she does seem dog mad at the moment, doesn't she?'

'She does, but right now is the worst

time in the world for us to think about getting one. With Christmas coming and a new baby we're going to be so busy and everything will be hectic. Puppies need a lot of attention. I'm afraid she's going to have to wait a while.' She shoved a cushion behind her back and settled herself more comfortably on the sofa. 'You're sure you didn't mind keeping me company, Izzy? I feel a bit mean that the rest of them are practically having a party at The Ducklings and you're stuck here with me, eating takeaway.'

'You must be joking!' Izzy was relieved she'd had an excuse to get away. 'Nell may have laid on a spread for them all, but she'll have Riley, Xander and Connor shifting furniture around, and Rachel will be dragged into hanging curtains and goodness knows what else, and young Sam will be making cups of tea. I'm well out of it. I'd much rather be sitting here with you and Michael Bublé, thank you very much.'

Anna laughed. 'It's nice, though, isn't it? To see Riley and Nell moving in together, I mean.' She pursed her lips, thinking. 'Crikey! Do you realise it's exactly one year ago tonight that they met? The night of the bonfire meal at The Bay Horse, remember?' She shook her head. 'That seems like ages ago.'

'It was,' Izzy pointed out. 'Three hundred and sixty-five days to be exact, as I well remember.'

Anna looked horrified. 'Oh, gosh, Izzy, I'm so sorry! I completely forgot!'

'Don't worry about it.'

'But I do worry about it! I can't believe I was so tactless. I'm such an idiot.'

'It's baby brain, probably,' Izzy said with a rueful smile. 'Honestly, forget it.'

So, it had been a year since she'd met Matt, too. At least, since she had met him *again* after years of him living away from the village. The son of Ernie and Sandra, who ran The Bay Horse, he'd moved back to the village after being made redundant from his job in

Birmingham. Having secured work in Whitby he'd intended to stay put in Bramblewick long-term. Well, she'd soon put a stop to that, hadn't she?

Anna was watching her, and Izzy could see the curiosity in her eyes. 'You're sure it's over? For good?'

'One hundred per cent positive,' Izzy assured her. She took a large gulp of her coffee, hoping Anna would drop the subject.

'I still can't get my head around it,' Anna said. 'You and Matt seemed so right for each other, and you were so happy. It's weird how it all just fizzled out.'

'Yes, well, it had been going wrong for a few months,' Izzy said uncomfortably. 'It was best all round when he said he'd found a flat in Whitby and was moving away.'

'Whitby's only a few miles away, though,' Anna pointed out. 'It didn't have to be the end of your relationship. I know he wanted to move out from the pub, but I don't understand why he didn't just move in with you at Rose Cottage. You *did* ask him?'

Izzy squirmed. 'I told you I did.'

'But it was obviously what he wanted,' Anna said. She frowned. 'During the summer, we were taking bets on who would ask who first. You both seemed so smitten with each other. I was predicting wedding bells.'

'Look, Anna, I told you. It didn't work out, that's all. We talked about him moving in and that led to — other things.'

'What other things?'

'You know. *The talk.* What do we want from this relationship? Where is it going? Where do we see ourselves in five years' time? That sort of stuff.'

Anna gave her a sympathetic look. 'And it went wrong from there?'

'And it went wrong from there,' Izzy agreed. *Hadn't it just!* 'When it came down to it, we wanted different things. We tried to pretend it would be all right, but it just never felt the same. We limped on for a few more months before we realised it wasn't fair on either of us. Everything had changed. It was time to let go.'

Anna sighed. 'I guess if you wanted a commitment and he didn't there wasn't a lot you could do about it. I'm sorry, Izzy.'

'It's not the end of the world,' Izzy said, forcing herself to sound cheerful. 'Who'd have thought I'd be the only single one in the group now, eh? Can't believe even Holls has got a boyfriend at last.'

Her ploy worked. Anna immediately began to talk about their friend Holly's new man, and how it was the first relationship Holly had embarked upon for five years. Izzy let her ramble on, glad that the subject had been changed. She didn't want to think about Matt, nor about the reasons their relationship had collapsed. It was, after all, entirely down to her.

★   ★   ★

'You know what this is about, don't you?' Ash raised an eyebrow as his colleague, Jackson Wade, murmured in his ear. 'If you've got any sense you'll have your excuses ready to blurt out before she gets the chance to say a word.'

The she in question, thought Ash, *being Mrs Morgan presumably*. As if Monday mornings weren't bad enough, the headmistress of Bramblewick Primary School had waltzed into the staffroom during break and called the staff to attention. Judging by the gloomy looks on everyone's faces, they'd all guessed the reason. It was, after all, that time of year again.

Sure enough, Mrs Morgan didn't beat around the bush. 'The Christmas play,' she said, watching them shrewdly as they all stared wide-eyed at her, like naughty schoolchildren awaiting punishment. 'We need to start making preparations. Choosing a play, for a start, and finding someone to take on the overall organisation. So, any volunteers?'

Ash wasn't the slightest bit surprised when a deathly silence ensued. It was pretty much par for the course. Everyone hated the job which was considered a lot of hard work that simply wasn't worth giving up precious free time for. It looked like this year was going to be the same as all the others then. He opened his mouth to volunteer, then snapped it shut again as a voice piped up, 'I'll do it.'

There was a surprised muttering as everyone looked around to see who'd been crazy enough to volunteer. Ash's eyes widened in amazement as he realised it was Isobel Clark who had offered. Izzy had never offered before. He wondered what had persuaded her this time.

Even Mrs Morgan seemed shocked. 'Are you sure, Izzy? It's a big undertaking. You have no experience, after all. Maybe you could work with someone else?' She looked appealingly at Ash. 'Someone who knows a bit more about this sort of thing?'

Okay, so that was practically begging. Ash rolled his eyes. 'I don't mind

11

helping her,' he heard himself saying and wondered why. He could have got out of it for once. Then again, hadn't he assumed he'd be doing it by himself anyway? That's what had happened for the last few years.

'You fool,' Jackson whispered into his coffee mug, presumably so Mrs Morgan wouldn't hear him.

Ash grinned at him. 'You do know I'll be roping you in to help?'

'You can try,' Jackson replied, sounding pretty convinced that it wouldn't work.

'That's splendid,' Mrs Morgan said, beaming at Ash and Izzy approvingly. 'You'll make the perfect team, I'm sure. And I know I don't have to tell you, Ash, what needs doing, so perhaps you'd be good enough to bring Isobel up to speed with the requirements. I'm sure I can leave it all in your capable hands.' She glanced at her watch. 'Goodness, break's almost over. I'll leave you to finish your drinks before you head back to your classrooms. Thank you.'

Taking the hint, the staff members immediately got busy. Some drained their cups, others headed to the sink to rinse their empty mugs under the tap, others filed out of the staff room.

'You must be mad. The best of British luck to you,' said Dawn Lewis, one of the younger teachers, as she walked past him on her way out.

He saw the grins on the faces of his colleagues and wondered what he'd done. His eyes met Izzy's and she shrugged, as if she was wondering the same. They were the last to leave the staff room, and Ash hovered uncertainly as he waited for her to rinse out her mug. 'You're sure about this?' he asked her as she finally put it on the draining board.

Izzy folded her arms, looking defiant. 'Don't you want my help?' she demanded.

Ash was a bit taken aback. 'It's not that at all. Anyway, it's me who'll be helping you. You're in charge this year, remember?'

'Oh, yeah,' she muttered. 'I'd forgotten that bit.'

'I take it you don't know much about running a school play?'

'I don't know anything about it really,' she admitted, as they headed out into the corridor, 'except it's a lot of hard work and takes up all your free time.'

'You're right about that,' he confirmed. 'So why volunteer?'

'Why do *you* volunteer every year?' she countered.

She had a point. Ash shrugged. 'Nothing better to do, I suppose.'

'Well, there you go then,' she said.

They looked at each other, and he felt there was a sudden unspoken acknowledgment between them that they were both failures who had no life outside of the school. But wasn't Izzy seeing that Matt Jones chap from The Bay Horse? Had been for months, as far as he was aware. What would he think if she was stuck in the school for the entire run-up to Christmas?

'What about your boyfriend?' he asked. 'Have you told him you'll be out of circulation for the next six weeks or so?'

He saw her eyes narrow. 'That's a bit sexist, isn't it?' she said. 'Even if I had a boyfriend — which for your information, I don't — it would be my business how I spent my spare time. I don't need anyone's permission, let alone a man's.'

Ash held up his hands. 'Sorry, you're absolutely right,' he admitted, thinking, *so she and Matt are over? When did that happen?* 'It's just — you do know how much work this involves, right?'

She pulled a face. 'Honestly? Not a clue. Still, I'm sure you'll be on hand to tell me, and I'm not afraid of hard work. How bad can it be?'

Ash looked at her thoughtfully. She tucked a strand of her short, bobbed blonde hair behind her ear and stared at him, defiance in her brown eyes. He wondered why she felt the sudden need to be busy and a memory came to him from his own past. How he'd thrown himself into work as a means of escape from all the hurt and misery. Clearly, she was heartbroken over this Matt fella. He couldn't blame her for wanting to think about something — anything — else.

'It's not bad at all,' he assured her gently. 'It's hard, yes, but it's fun, too, and very rewarding. The kids love it and it really does bring out the best in them. I think those members of staff who refuse point blank to have anything to do with it are missing out, quite honestly.'

Izzy looked at him as if she was trying to work out if he was genuine or not. 'O-kay,' she said at last. 'Where do we start?'

He glanced at his watch. 'We're due in class,' he pointed out. 'Meet me in the staff room at lunch and we'll start making plans.'

'Will do,' she said. As she moved away, she tapped him on his arm. 'Just remember,' she added, 'I'm in charge and you're my lackey.'

His eyes widened in surprise and she grinned. 'Kidding,' she said and headed off down the corridor. 'See you later,' she called over her shoulder and he raised a hand in awkward acknowledgement, wondering how this new partnership was going to pan out. He was used to working alone. He was used to *being* alone. This was going to be a very different experience. How ironic that it was Izzy, of all people, that he was going to be sharing it with.

2

'I can't believe you were crazy enough to volunteer!' Anna shook her head, seeming dazed at the very idea of her friend taking on a huge project like Bramblewick Primary School's Christmas play.

Izzy felt offended. 'I don't see what's so weird about it. Ash does it every year, after all.'

'Exactly!' Anna exclaimed. '*Ash does it every year.* On his own. With no help from you. And, it has to be said, it works. He's such a good teacher and really knows how to get the best out of his pupils. Why on earth would you interfere with that?'

'Oh, thanks very much for that,' Izzy said.

Connor burst out laughing. 'I don't think she meant it that way,' he assured her, casting an affectionate glance at his wife, who was sitting on the sofa looking a bit, thought Izzy grumpily, like Humpty Dumpty about to fall off his wall. 'I think she just meant, *if it ain't broke why fix it?* Ash seems to know what he's doing, and I thought you tried to avoid getting involved, anyway?'

'She did!' Anna said. 'She always said she'd never get bogged down in all that awful Christmas play stuff and that Ash must be either a nutcase or a martyr. You did!' she added, as Izzy opened her mouth to protest. 'Don't try to deny it.'

'I wasn't going to deny it,' Izzy said. 'I just thought, why should Ash always have to give up his free time? It's time someone else did their share and, as no one else stepped forward, I volunteered.'

'But Ash is helping out anyway?' said Riley, sounding puzzled.

'Yes. The idiot volunteered to assist me, after all that sacrifice on my part. You just can't help some people.' She sighed. 'I really don't know how this is going to pan out, you know. He went over a load of stuff in break yesterday morning and it seems like an awful lot of work. Maybe I was a bit hasty.'

'Too late now,' Rachel said, coming in from the kitchen of Folly Farm with plates of sliced pizza in her hands. Behind her, Xander, her partner, carried dishes of nachos and dips. 'You're in it up to your neck, and whether it's too much work or not you're going to have to get on with it.'

'Maybe Xander could help us out?' Izzy said, eyeing him hopefully.

The man in question laughed as he placed the dishes on the coffee table then sank onto the sofa. 'Sorry, Izzy. Even if I wanted to, you know I'm heading back south tomorrow for work. I won't be back until Christmas week and it will be too late by then.'

'Don't remind me,' Rachel said, sounding gloomy. 'All those weeks without you.'

'I'll get back whenever I can,' he promised her. 'And there's always video calling.'

Xander was a successful actor who was currently working on the final series of his hit show, *Lord Curtis Investigates*. He'd agreed to bring the programme to its satisfactory conclusion but was then planning to give up television and film work to concentrate on local theatre, and to help run the unofficial animal sanctuary that Folly Farm had recently turned into. Rachel, who worked as practice nurse at Bramblewick Surgery, had known he was contracted to finish the show when they embarked on their relationship, but it didn't make saying goodbye to him any easier. She'd decided to throw him a farewell dinner before he left — just a quiet night at home with pizza and snacks for their friends. Izzy could see in her face that she was already missing him. She could relate to that, she thought sadly.

It was weird, being the only single one in the group. Even Rachel's mum had recently paired up with her friend, elderly vet Merlyn. The two of them had gone out to the pictures that very evening, taking Rachel's son Sam with them. Izzy felt totally out of place, especially now her terminally-single friend Holly was dating.

'Where's Holly?' she asked, realising that their pal hadn't turned up.

'Not coming,' Rachel said. 'She's spending the evening with Jonathan.'

'Oh!' Anna rolled her eyes. 'The famous Jonathan.'

'Have you met him yet?' Izzy enquired, reaching out for a slice of pizza.

'No one's met him,' Anna said. 'Something dodgy about him, if you ask me.'

'Anna!' Nell burst out laughing. 'What happened to the fair-minded, kind-hearted receptionist we all used to know and love?'

'Hormones,' Connor said. 'She just says it like it is these days, believe me.'

Anna frowned. 'I'm not being mean. I'm just giving my opinion. Why hasn't Holly introduced him to us? There's something — not right about it.'

'I've been thinking the same thing,' Rachel admitted. 'She's waited long enough to get a boyfriend, I'd have thought she'd have been straight round to show him off. I'm hoping I'm wrong about him.'

'In what way?' Xander said, sounding curious.

Rachel shrugged, as if unwilling to continue the conversation.

Anna clearly wasn't so reluctant. 'I reckon he's married,' she announced.

They all looked at each other, their mutual unease apparent.

'I'm sure he's not,' Connor said eventually. 'We hardly know the chap. Need to give him a chance, at least.'

'And Holly seems blissfully happy,' Nell added. 'They're probably so loved up they don't need anyone else right now.'

'I suppose so,' Anna said, sounding unconvinced. 'Anyway, enough of this. Izzy, don't keep that cheese pizza to yourself! Pass me a slice, or three.'

'Do you want some of the pep-peroni?'

'Gosh, no.' Anna pulled a face. 'I get terrible heartburn. I'll probably get it anyway, come to think of it, but it will be so worth it. This all looks fabulous and I'm starving.'

'Didn't Gracie want to come?' Nell asked, scooping some cream cheese and chive dip onto a small plate and grabbing a handful of nachos to go with it. 'Although, I don't think she'd eat this sort of stuff anyway, would she?'

Connor shook his head. 'Doesn't like messy food,' he explained. 'She's much happier at home watching DVDs with Jane. Jacko's there, too, so she's in a very good mood.'

'I think it's great that the mother of Anna's ex-boyfriend is so close to you all,' Rachel said, sounding awestruck. 'I can't imagine Grant's mother bothering with me. She doesn't even bother with her own grandson. Not that I mind. She's a vile woman.'

'Jane's lovely. We've always got on.

Julian, her husband, even gave me away at my wedding,' Anna told her. 'They've really taken to Gracie, and she adores Jacko. I think he's the reason she wants a puppy of her own.'

'Are you going to get her one?' Riley asked, pinching some of Nell's nachos and earning a reproachful stare from her.

'Not for a good while,' Connor said. 'We've got enough on our plates at the moment, and if we do it certainly won't be a border collie like Jacko. Far too energetic for us.'

Izzy swallowed the last of her pizza and leaned back against the chair. 'So, have any of you got any tips for me? Rachel, Anna, your kids will more than likely be involved in this play, after all. And, Xander, whether you're going to be here or not you know your stuff about theatre productions.'

'My biggest tip,' Xander said, 'would be to keep it simple.'

'And mine,' Connor added, raising an eyebrow, 'would be to make sure

Gracie gets a part, because if she's not up on that stage at some point she'll be furious, and our lives won't be worth living.'

Izzy laughed but she knew he wasn't really joking. Gracie was on the autism spectrum, and her passion for singing and dancing knew no bounds. She would never understand if she didn't get a part in the play. Not that there was any probability that she'd be left out. She was very talented and had a real gift for learning her lines, too. Gracie wouldn't be the problem, she thought ruefully. How to include as many children from the school as possible? And how to fit in rehearsals for everyone?

'Which play are you doing?' Xander queried.

'Well, that's the thing, we haven't decided yet. Ash showed me a website that you can buy plays from. It's ever so good. You get all the scripts and the soundtrack and everything. It's where he usually gets them from every year.

But, as he said, most of them are for fairly narrow age groups and we want to try to include children from each year, from nursery age up to the kids who'll be heading off to secondary school next autumn. We're going to have to make up some stuff for those who fall outside the age range.'

'Or just get them to sing?' Riley suggested. 'Och, my wee nephews were stars at their Christmas play the other year. Fair broke my heart hearing them sing some Christmas carols.'

'You're such a softie,' Nell said, nudging him affectionately. 'He's right though,' she told Izzy. 'There's nothing says Christmas like children singing carols.'

'I know, and they probably will at some point, but I think they'd like to do a bit of acting, too. Oh, well, I'll have a browse on the website tomorrow and see if I can find something I like.'

'And that Ash likes,' Rachel pointed out.

'Ash will have to like what I like,' Izzy

said firmly. 'He's my assistant. Not the other way around.'

Anna gave her a knowing look. 'Is Ash seeing anyone, by the way?'

Izzy pulled a face. 'I have no idea and I don't care one way or the other. You can get that idea out of your head. Ash is a colleague, nothing else. Work and play definitely don't mix.'

'Oh, I wouldn't say that,' Connor said, smiling at Anna. 'Sometimes they mix very well indeed.'

'And Ash is wonderful,' Anna continued eagerly. 'He's so good with Gracie. She was very upset when she had to leave his class to move up to Miss Robson's, but he assured her she could come to him any time if she had a worry or a problem. She knows he's still there for her and it's made all the difference.'

'He is a good teacher,' Izzy acknowledged. 'I've never said he isn't. And he's a nice man, too, I'm not disputing that. All I'm saying is, he's a workmate and nothing more, so please don't be getting any ideas in that direction. Besides, don't you think it's a bit soon? I've only just broken up with Matt. Give me time to wallow, for goodness sake.'

'You said you and Matt were over months ago, unofficially,' Anna pointed out. 'All right, all right.' She held up her hands in defeat. 'Not another word, I promise.'

'Good,' Izzy said. 'Now, can we get back to enjoying our food? This is Xander's last night here for weeks, so I think it's Rachel you should be worrying about. She's going to be a right misery guts from tomorrow, whereas I'll be knee deep in work and small children and won't have time to think about men at all. I know who I'd rather be!'

★   ★   ★

The staffroom was quiet and empty but for Ash and Izzy, who sat, hands furled around mugs of coffee, staring at the laptop on the table in front of them.

'So, we're agreed we're not doing the Nativity?' Ash was doubtful. 'It might be the best thing, you know. You're new to all this and it's such a well-known and well-loved production.'

'I know that, but I'd like to try something different. Anyway, you haven't staged a Nativity for years!'

'No, but I do always include carols at some point. The parents like it, and it's not really Christmas without the carols.'

'You sound like my friends,' Izzy said with a sigh. 'I'm thinking something new and exciting. Something contemporary. Something that people will talk about for years to come.'

'You don't want much, do you?' Ash said with a laugh. 'Thing is, Izzy, parents expect traditional at this time of year. They like to go home feeling all warm and cosy and festive. You can't just land something like *The Elf from Outer Space* on them.'

Izzy's eyes widened. '*The Elf from Outer Space?* Is that a real thing?'

Ash grinned. 'Who knows? Wouldn't surprise me. You should see some of the titles on this website I use. Some of our parents would have a fit.'

'What I want,' Izzy said with a sigh, 'is something that would fit with all the different age groups. Most of these plays are for ages seven to nine, or nine to eleven, or three to six or similar. How do you manage to find something for all the kids?'

'You don't have to,' Ash said patiently. 'Look, with the best will in the world, not every child is going to be able to take part in this play. It's just not feasible. What you can do is get the whole school involved in other ways.'

'Such as?'

'Singing, for one thing. Costume making. Scenery. Props. They love it. And the parents are just as thrilled to know that the star of the show is wearing a costume that their little darling sewed or glued something onto as they would be if the child was actually wearing it. All contributors are credited in the programme and that's enough for most of the adults. Then you get them all singing carols, class by class, at the end or during breaks in the play and everyone's happy.'

'What about a pantomime?' Izzy mused. 'Something like *Cinderella*, or *Aladdin*?'

'You have to be realistic,' Ash cautioned. 'Bear in mind the limits of our budget, and the costumes and scenery these things would involve.' He tapped the screen. 'See? We need to find something where costumes will need minimum creation and scenery will be extremely basic.'

'May as well stick with a carol concert then,' Izzy said gloomily. 'This is a nightmare.' She brightened suddenly. 'Unless!'

Ash frowned. 'Unless what?'

'We make it a contemporary pantomime. You know, Cinderella isn't going to a ball but a school disco. The prince isn't a prince but the coolest boy in school. That sort of thing.'

Ash tried not to sound appalled. 'Are you serious?'

'We could make it a Christmas disco,' Izzy continued. 'It wouldn't take much to make the hall look festive, since it's already decorated every year anyway. The kids could just come in their best clothes. It wouldn't cost us anything.'

'Izzy, I think that sounds awful,' Ash said bluntly.

Izzy glared at him. 'Well, you're my assistant remember? It's my decision at the end of the day, not yours.'

'Yeah, I get that, but honestly. I think the parents will be pretty miffed, and the kids will be disappointed. They like to dress up. They want something magical, not based on reality. Who wants to see a Christmas play set in the very school hall that they'll actually be performing in?'

'I'm being practical, like you told me,' she pointed out.

'I understand that, but there's being practical and being dull as ditch water. You need a sprinkling of festive magic or no one will want to be involved at all.'

Izzy shrugged. 'I haven't finalised it yet, but I'll think of something to add some sparkle.'

Ash couldn't believe what he was hearing. 'You're seriously thinking about this?'

Izzy sipped her coffee, eyeing him coldly. 'Why not? I haven't heard anything better from you.'

'Because I daren't open my mouth. Everything I suggested was shot down in flames by you yesterday. All my ideas are too boring and predictable, remember?'

'You said it,' Izzy said with a scowl.

The door was pushed open and Jackson Wade strolled in. 'You two still here? I was just going home and saw the light. That's dedication.' He grinned at them. 'So, is it all going well?'

Izzy and Ash glared at him and he burst out laughing. 'Clearly not. Told you not to volunteer, didn't I?' he said, nodding at Ash.

'Wish he'd taken your advice,' Izzy muttered.

Ash tutted. 'We can't agree on a play,' he said.

Jackson whistled. 'You haven't even got that far? Blimey, it's going to be Easter before it's ready, at this rate. What's the problem?'

'He's a boring stick-in-the-mud,' Izzy said, poking Ash in the arm with unnecessary force.

Ash rolled his eyes. 'She's got some crazy idea about a Cinderella set in a contemporary school with a Christmas disco instead of a ball. What do you think of that?'

Jackson wrinkled his nose. 'Sounds awful.'

'See!' Ash couldn't keep the triumphant note out of his voice. 'I told you!'

'Well, he would side with you, wouldn't he?' Izzy said. 'All boys together. Perish the thought that a woman should be in charge for once.'

'Oh no you don't.' Ash shook his head. 'Don't you dare play the sexism card with me. I'm happy for you to take charge and I'm happy to assist you, but don't make out that I'm trying to take over just because I'm a man.'

'So, what are you doing?'

'Trying to help! For goodness sake, Izzy, this is a magical once-a-year production that all the kids and parents look forward to. They want to be transported somewhere else, not dumped back in the school hall. You must see that?'

'No, I don't. And I think you're being very short-sighted and negative,' Izzy said, collecting her laptop. 'I'm taking this home with me and I shall have a look through and make a decision. Tonight. And tomorrow, I shall inform you which play we're performing, and that's final.'

Ash sighed as she stalked out of the staff room, slamming the door behind her.

'What's up with her?' Jackson demanded. 'Bit bossy, isn't she?'

'I have a feeling she's working to forget something — or someone. I really hope this isn't going to be a total disaster.'

Jackson raised an eyebrow. 'You can walk away, you know. It's not compulsory. You can tell the head that you're not comfortable working with Izzy and that you'd rather not be involved.'

'But she hasn't got a clue what she's doing.'

'That's her problem.'

Jackson, thought Ash, saw things very simply. He liked to compartmentalize, keep things neat and tidy in his life and in his mind. There was no room for chaos in any form. He wouldn't understand Ash's dilemma at all. 'I can't just leave her to cope alone, and who else is going to offer? No one, that's who.'

'And like I said — '

'I know what you said, but it's not just her problem is it? What about all the kids who look forward to this play every year? What about the parents who expect to sit through a show each Christmas? I can't disappoint them.'

'You know your trouble, Ash?' Jackson said, shaking his head. 'You're way too nice.'

'I know,' Ash said with a wry smile. 'So people keep telling me. It's a curse.'

Jackson put his arm around him. 'Tell you what, mate, come back to mine for your tea. We can have a good moan together.'

'And you might be able to help me come up with an idea for the play?'

Jackson groaned. 'Let's not go that far, but who knows? Come on. We'll call at the Indian takeaway in Helmston. There's no problem so great that a nice chicken bhuna can't solve it.'

* * *

Ash couldn't, in all honesty, say he was looking forward to that evening. He'd promised to meet Izzy at her home straight after school, and she had promised she would unveil this year's Bramblewick Primary School Christmas production to him. What would it be? *Cinderella Goes to the School Disco? Aladdin and the Genie of the iPad? Puss in Converse Trainers?*

He took a deep breath as he pushed open the gate to Rose Cottage and walked down the path. The pale blue door had a large brass door knocker, and he lifted it and rapped with more force than he'd intended, almost as if he was making a statement that he wasn't worried, and Izzy didn't intimidate him in the slightest.

'You have to stop taking all this so personally,' Jackson had advised him last night, and Ash knew he was right. After all, how bad could things be? It was just a school play, and Izzy was a decent enough person. Deep down. Somewhere inside.

'Come in!' Izzy beamed at him as she opened the door and ushered him into the small square that passed as a hall.

As she closed the front door behind him, Ash felt an immense heat that made him immediately unbutton his coat. Izzy led the way into a small, cosy living room, and he saw the source of the heat was a wood burning stove, tucked into a large brick fireplace.

'Here, let me take that,' Izzy said, holding out her hands for the coat. He removed it gratefully and handed it over. She opened the door to a cupboard under the stairs where, hopefully, there was a coat hook, then headed into what he assumed was the kitchen. 'Cup of tea?' she called. 'Or would you prefer something stronger? There's wine, or beer if you'd prefer?'

Ash decided it was probably best he kept a clear head. 'Tea would be fine,' he assured her, settling himself on the sofa and looking around him approvingly. Izzy's home was a proper country cottage, he thought, with old beams and a large brick fireplace and white-washed walls. He loved it. It had so much more character than his flat in Helmston. It was the sort of place where you could really be comfortable, somewhere to make a home in.

'Sugar? Milk?' Her voice drifted into

his thoughts and he blinked.

'What? Oh, milk please. No sugar.'

She was back within a couple of minutes, carrying a tray bearing two mugs of tea and a plate of chocolate biscuits which she placed on the coffee table. She tucked her hair behind her ears and waved a hand over the tray. 'Help yourself. Doesn't matter which mug you choose. We both take our tea the same way.'

Was that a good omen, he wondered. At least they had one thing in common. He braced himself for her answer as he posed the question finally. 'So, have you chosen a play?'

'I have.' She reached for a chocolate biscuit then sat on the armchair, curling her feet beneath her and watching him through innocent-looking eyes.

Ash wasn't fooled. 'Go on then.'

Izzy leaned forward, waving her biscuit in the air, her face eager. 'Are you ready for this? *Little Red in the Hood*. A tale of inner-city innocence destroyed by the capitalist wolves. A moral story of Christmas commercialism and how it ruins the festive spirit.'

Ash heard a plop and realised half of his biscuit had dropped into his cup of tea. He snapped his mouth shut, then fished around in the mug. Rescuing the soggy mess from the liquid before it disintegrated completely, he put it back on the plate and apologised, then pleaded, 'You *are* joking, right?'

For a moment she glared at him then, to his enormous relief, her eyes crinkled in the corners and she threw back her head and laughed. 'Your face! Of course I'm joking, you banana. As if!'

Ash realised he'd been holding his breath and exhaled. 'Well, after what you said last night . . . '

'Oh, you just annoyed me last night,' she said, waving a dismissive hand at him. 'You and that control freak Jackson Wade. I was winding you up, but you did deserve it, you know. Just remember, I'm in charge and you're — '

'Just your assistant,' Ash finished for

her. 'Yes, I know. So, have you actually come up with a play or not?'

'I have, honestly.' Izzy suddenly looked rather nervous, which endeared her to him immediately. Not quite the dictator she appeared, then. 'It's a bit of a mashup.'

'A mashup?' Ash frowned. 'Go on, spill.'

'Okay.' Izzy held up her hands. 'Hear me out on this, 'cos I really do think it could work. It's a play I spotted online, and it's got all new songs and lots of parts for kids in a wide age range, and I think there's scope to add a few of the younger ones in, too. It's *A Christmas Carol* crossed with *Oliver Twist*, and it's called *A Twisted Christmas*.'

Ash's eyes widened. 'What?'

'Don't say it like that! In this version, Ebenezer Scrooge is the owner of an orphanage, and instead of Tiny Tim there's poor little Orphan Oliver. I was thinking we could have lots of the nursery class involved as other little orphans. They wouldn't have to say much, but we could have a scene with them queuing for their dinner or in bed in the dormitory when the first ghost appears — '

'I love it!'

Izzy stared at him. 'You do?'

'Yes, I really do. What a great idea. It's traditional enough for the parents, has lots of Christmassy elements, but is something new and different at the same time. Brilliant, Izzy!'

'Oh, well.' She looked quite stunned that he'd accepted her choice so easily, but Ash's mind was already whirring with possibilities. 'You say there's a whole new soundtrack included?'

'Yeah. I was listening to some of the songs last night online — just excerpts but enough to know that the kids could manage them easily enough. I thought we could add in some traditional carols, too, so the audience could join in. You know how much parents love 'Away in a Manger'.'

'There's never a dry eye in the house,' he agreed, smiling. 'This is going to be great. Did you buy the licence for it?'

She shook her head. 'I was waiting to see what you thought of the idea first,' she admitted.

He gave her a meaningful look. 'Me? But I'm just the assistant, remember?'

'Yeah, yeah. I know. So, you think we should go for it?'

'Absolutely! You get your laptop and we'll crack on with it right now. I gave you our school account details, didn't I?'

'You did, but why don't you order it and I'll make us both another cup of tea? Actually, since it's gone six, do you want to stay for something to eat? I haven't had tea yet and I'm starving. I could rustle something up for us.'

He was about to tell her not to bother, but his stomach rumbled, reminding him that he was pretty hungry, too. 'If you're sure you don't mind?'

'I've got a craving for sausages and mash,' she said. 'Comfort food. Would that be okay with you?'

Ash couldn't wipe the smile from his face. 'It's my absolute favourite meal.'

'Really? Mine, too! Okay, I'll just get you the laptop then I'll start cooking.'

'Do you need any help?'

'No, of course not. You just sort out the play and I'll make the tea. We've got an awful lot of work to get through. Best fuel up, don't you think?'

3

Helmston Market was heaving, and Izzy was beginning to wonder if it had been such a good idea to go shopping that afternoon, after all. It wasn't too bad for her, but for Anna it must be exhausting. Despite her friend's insistence that she was absolutely fine, Izzy wasn't so sure.

'I think we should find a cafe,' she said, noting the weary look on Anna's face.

'I don't need to stop,' Anna protested, as Izzy had suspected she would.

'Maybe you don't, but I do. I'm shattered. I need a sit down,' Izzy said firmly. Anna could be very stubborn sometimes, but Connor wouldn't thank her if she allowed his very pregnant wife to tramp around the market all afternoon without making sure she rested. 'It's much busier than I expected it to be. And how come most of these stalls are already decked out for Christmas? They do know it's still only November?'

Anna laughed. 'Some of them were decorated in October. Where have you been?'

'Up to my neck in marking and lesson planning,' Izzy reminded her. 'And it's only going to get worse from now. Come on, let's go to the Castle Keep Cafe and get a nice hot chocolate. I need something to defrost me.'

Since Helmston's pride and joy was its medieval castle ruins, it was difficult to find any business not named after its castle in one form or another. The Castle Keep Cafe wasn't the only one of the many teashops that cashed in on the popularity of the town's number one tourist attraction, but since it was a pretty building and served good food at a reasonable price, it was one of the most well-known ones. As it was late afternoon, many people had already eaten, or were saving themselves for tea, so it wasn't as busy as it had been an hour or two earlier when Anna and Izzy had first passed it.

They chose a table by the window and Anna managed to squeeze herself into the chair. Izzy eyed her warily.

'Are you sure you're okay?'

Anna rolled her eyes. 'Please, don't start. I get enough of this from Connor every day. Let's have a look at that menu.'

They decided on toasted teacakes and mugs of hot chocolate, and after the waitress came to take their order, they leaned back in their chairs and gave sighs of relief. The flames from the open fire at one end of the room soon warmed them up enough that they could finally remove their coats and scarves, placing them on a spare chair.

'I don't get why so many people are already Christmas shopping,' Izzy grumbled, staring out of the window at the crowds of people in the narrow street outside, struggling under the weight of carrier bags.

'Like me, you mean?' Anna said with a grin, nodding at the carrier bags she'd stuffed under the table.

'Not at all,' Izzy protested. 'It's obvious why you're Christmas shopping early. All being well, by Christmas week you'll be in the hospital making a special delivery of your own. What's their excuse?'

'Aw, I think it's nice,' Anna said. 'I like the Christmas build-up. Come to think of it, you always did, too. What happened to my jolly festive pal?' She frowned. 'Is this because of Matt?'

Izzy sighed. 'No, it's not. I'm over Matt.'

Anna didn't look convinced. 'Really? So soon?' She shook her head. 'I can't believe he didn't want to get serious. He seemed so keen back in the summer. What a louse.'

'It's not what you think,' Izzy said, feeling uncomfortable. 'You've got him all wrong. I can't let him take the blame, because it wasn't his fault. It was mine.'

'Yours?' Anna frowned. 'But you wanted him to move into Rose Cottage with you, didn't you?'

'Yes of course I did.' Izzy wished Anna would just drop the subject. 'That wasn't the issue.'

'Then what was the issue?' Anna persisted. She smiled at the waitress, who had returned with their order. For a few minutes, conversation was suspended as they buttered teacakes and stirred hot chocolate and settled back in their chairs. Izzy, however, knew that Anna wouldn't let it drop and she was right.

'Come on, Izz. You've been my best friend for like — forever. We always tell each other everything. What went wrong, really?'

Izzy took a sip of hot chocolate, playing for time. She realised she wasn't going to get away with evasive action for much longer. Anna was nothing if not determined — and terminally nosy when it came to her friends. She didn't mean any harm by it, Izzy realised. It

51

was just Anna's nature to want her friends to be happy, and she always thought that if she knew the situation she could somehow fix things for them. Well, she was wrong. There was no fixing this.

'So, you had the talk . . . ' Anna began. Her voice trailed off as she waited for Izzy to continue.

Izzy sighed. 'Yes, we had the talk. I asked him about moving into Rose Cottage and he was all for it. Somehow, and I'm not even sure how, it turned into a conversation about the future and about what we wanted from our relationship. And that's when it all came out — the fact that we clearly wanted different things.'

'But what did you want that he didn't?' Anna said, puzzled. 'Was it marriage? Was he against the idea?'

'Not at all. We both agreed that it was something we'd like at some point — a few years down the line. It wasn't marriage we disagreed on. It was kids.'

'Kids!' Anna let out a sharp breath.

'Oh, golly. So, Matt doesn't want kids? I'm so sorry, Izzy. How weird. I'd have thought he'd have made a great father, too. He's so good with Gracie and Sam, isn't he? What a shame.'

Izzy blinked away tears and blew on her hot chocolate. 'Anna, stop it. It's not Matt who doesn't want kids. It's me.'

If she'd announced that she didn't want to live in Bramblewick anymore and was planning to set up home in an igloo somewhere in the Arctic circle, Anna couldn't have looked more shocked.

Her friend practically dropped the mug of hot chocolate she was holding and stared at Izzy in amazement. 'You don't want kids? But — but of course you do. You've always wanted kids!'

Izzy raised an eyebrow. 'Really? Since when?'

Anna looked totally bewildered. 'But you're — you're a *teacher*!'

Izzy almost burst out laughing at her evident bafflement. 'What's that got to do with anything?'

'You're so good with children,' Anna said. 'And you're surrounded by them every day. I don't understand. I thought you loved kids.'

'I do love kids,' Izzy said, realising that Anna was falling into the same trap that her own mother had fallen into when she'd explained how she felt to her, several years ago. At least, she'd tried to explain it to her, but her mother had been so horrified, so appalled that her daughter didn't feel in the slightest bit inclined to have her own family, that they'd had a huge argument.

Even now, she seemed unable to accept it, making pointed comments about Izzy's biological clock ticking. Mostly, Izzy ignored it, but sometimes she'd try to explain again and there would inevitably be cross words. It was the only thing they ever argued about. Izzy knew her mum loved her and only wanted her to be happy. She just wished she could accept that Izzy could be perfectly happy as a childless woman, but that seemed like an impossible dream.

It was what she'd been afraid of with Anna, and all her other friends. For some reason, people seemed to assume that not wanting children of her own meant that she didn't like them. It wasn't the case at all. 'I like being around them. I like spending time with them. I just don't want any of my own. Is that so hard to understand?'

Anna looked as if she didn't know how to respond. Izzy tried hard not to feel hurt, but she could feel the discomfort growing and tears pricked at her eyes. 'I thought you'd at least try to understand.'

'I am trying,' Anna assured her. 'Honestly, Izzy, it's just that — well, it never occurred to me, that's all. I'm just surprised.' She sipped her hot chocolate, eyeing her friend warily. 'Maybe if you didn't work with them all day you'd want some of your own?'

Izzy groaned inwardly. Why were

people always trying to think of reasons why she didn't want children? She never asked them to explain why they *did*, did she? 'Even if I wasn't a teacher, I still wouldn't have children,' she said firmly. 'I love my job. I love working with youngsters, nurturing them. That doesn't change anything. It's just not something I've ever thought was in my future. I don't know why. I don't feel any desire, whatsoever, to be a mother.'

'And Matt wanted to be a father?' Anna sighed. 'Poor Matt.'

Oh, so it's poor Matt now, is it? Izzy felt desperately hurt. 'So now you see why we had to break up.' She bit into her toasted teacake and chewed it determinedly, willing herself not to cry.

'But, maybe if you'd given it a go — living together, I mean — you might have changed your mind a few years down the line,' Anna said. Who knows?

'Or Matt might have changed his mind?' Izzy ventured.

'Well . . . ' Anna hesitated. 'I wouldn't have thought so.'

'No, I didn't think you would,' Izzy snapped. 'Basically, I'm a freak who should want children, and if I don't then there's something very wrong with me.'

'That's not what I'm saying,' Anna protested. She reached out and her hand covered Izzy's. 'I'm sorry. I didn't mean to upset you. It was just a surprise, that's all. It never occurred to me — '

'No, well. Now you know.'

'Yes, I do. And it's fine. Of course it is. You're entitled to make your own decisions, Izz. I respect that, and I won't push you about it again.'

She smiled uncertainly, cradling her hot chocolate in her other hand. Izzy gave her a weak smile.

'Fair enough. Hurry up and eat your teacake. It's getting cold.'

Anna nodded and did as she was told, and conversation switched to more mundane matters, but deep down, Izzy was a swirling mess of mixed emotions. Anna had been her best friend for so long, but now it felt as if something had changed irrevocably between them. She wished she'd never confided in her.

★ ★ ★

Dawn Lewis glanced around her classroom as the children huddled in pairs, working on the task that she and Izzy had set them. 'Remind me again why you volunteered for this.'

Izzy smiled. 'Believe it or not, it's not that bad. Although, to be fair, I had serious doubts this morning.'

Hadn't she just!

Izzy watched the pupils who were busy practising the improvised scenarios she and Dawn had allocated to them and remembered how she'd felt at nine-thirty when she'd visited Jackson Wade's class — the first class on her round. It had been so daunting, and she'd wished, with all her heart, that she'd thought it through before she opened her big, fat mouth.

Funny how, just a couple of hours

later, she was feeling more confident both in herself and in the children. A strange feeling of optimism had settled on her. Who would have thought it?

'It's true, it always comes right in the end,' Dawn conceded. 'And I love the way you get a feel for the kids' abilities by doing this. Better than formal auditions, I think.'

Izzy knew she was right. Every year, Ash visited each classroom in turn and got the children to pair up. He'd then give them two characters he wanted them to play. Each pair would decide between themselves who'd be playing which part, then they'd improvise a scene. It was always set up as a fun exercise, but Ash was really taking notes and deciding who could act and who should get the lead roles in the play. It had seemed harmless enough to Izzy when she was just a classroom teacher, observing the process, but knowing that she was now the one responsible for making the decisions she'd felt unaccountably nervous.

'I suppose this is how Simon Cowell must feel,' she'd muttered to Jackson.

His mouth had twitched in amusement. 'I hardly think so! Keep a sense of perspective, Izzy. It's just a school play.'

Huh! Easy for him to say, Izzy had thought glumly, remembering with some trepidation what Ash had told her that morning before the bell rang.

'We must try to get as many of the kids involved as we possibly can,' he'd said. 'Anyone who wants to be part of this should get the chance, one way or the other. Even if it's printing tickets. Anything, so long as they feel involved.'

Izzy had thought that it was a steep task. 'Luckily, not everyone wants to be involved,' she'd said, with some relief. 'Most of my class look bored at the very idea of it.'

He grinned. 'Yeah, well, your class is at that awkward stage.'

'Awkward stage?'

'Where everything is just so uncool and boring,' he said. 'Surely, you must remember that stage yourself?'

'Certainly not. I was always a very bright and interested child.'

'Sure you were,' he replied, and she laughed.

'All right, maybe not. It's a bit frustrating, though. They're at just the right age to actually put some real feeling into their lines, and to remember them well. Not like the younger ones. It's going to be quite a challenge to get them to concentrate on anything for long.'

'You'll be surprised,' Ash had assured her. 'The little ones really do get involved and very excited about it all. Some of them take it very seriously. And don't forget, some of them already attend dance class outside of school and are familiar with the concept of performing in front of an audience.'

'Like Gracie,' Izzy said, thinking of her friend's stepdaughter. 'You wouldn't believe how much she changes when she's on stage, would you?'

'I was thinking,' Ash ventured, 'that

she could be the Ghost of Christmas Present. What do you think?'

Izzy considered. The role in question would suit Gracie, she realised. Not only was it a fairly large speaking part, but there was a solo for Gracie to sing, too, as well as the job of leading the choir in a carol. As roles went it was probably one of the best in the play. 'She'll have to audition,' she pointed out. 'It wouldn't be fair otherwise.'

'Obviously,' he agreed. 'But I'll bet she's head and shoulders above any of the others. You just watch. And speaking of auditions . . . '

Which was when he'd reminded her of his usual method of casting for the major roles, and Izzy had found herself agreeing to go from classroom to classroom, holding undercover auditions. She'd left her own class in the capable hands of Caroline, her teaching assistant, who she'd already talked into helping out whenever and however she could. Ash said Jackson had reluctantly agreed to help out, too, as had several of the other teachers and TAs.

There was so much more to it than Izzy had realised and, not for the first time, she wondered if she'd done the right thing in volunteering. The only consolation she had was that Ash was her wingman. She couldn't imagine how he'd done it all those years without an assistant. He really was the most amazing teacher.

'I think they've had enough practice now,' Dawn whispered.

Izzy blinked, realising she'd been miles away. Dawn was right. The children had been practising for ages and they must surely have come up with something by now. She and Ash had decided on the characters of a street urchin and a rich nobleman or woman, and each pair of children were asked to choose which of those roles they would like to play, then had to act out an improvised five-minute scene. Between Ash and herself, several classes had already been visited, and the two of them had separately watched dozens of pairs of children acting out their scenes, many of them with amazing flair. As predicted, there had also been some truly dreadful acting, appalling accents, and, in too many cases, not much at all other than stifled giggles or open shrieks of laughter.

It was very easy to tell the ones who went to dance class, or those who genuinely wanted to be in the school play and took it all very seriously. There were some who only wanted to take part as a way of getting out of lessons, but a good proportion were really eager to be in the production, even though they weren't yet aware of which play they would be acting in. Izzy had already become adept at ascertaining which of the children were truly interested.

She and Dawn settled themselves on chairs and watched as, pair by pair, the children performed their little sketches. It was quite astonishing how talented some of the kids were; able to put on the most extraordinary accents and acquire funny little mannerisms that made the characters come to life before her eyes. What had struck her, more than anything, as she made her way around the school, was how much fun the children found it. She watched as, eyes shining, they stood before her, lost in the moment as they became cockney urchins, begging for a crust of bread, or imperious aristocrats, looking down their noses at the peasants before them.

How did they do that at such a young age, she wondered, impressed. Against all her expectations, with each classroom she visited, a feeling of excitement and joy had unfurled within her, drowning out her worries and anxieties about the technicalities of staging the play, squashing her concerns about the time it was going to take up, until she began to understand why Ash volunteered each year.

More than anything, she was grateful that it was taking her mind off Matt and staving off the feeling of loneliness that had threatened to swamp her just a few weeks ago. As she and Dawn exchanged murmured comments and made brief notes, Izzy decided that taking on the school play was probably the best decision she'd made in ages. She just hoped she could do it justice.

4

Anna hadn't wanted a baby shower, but her friends weren't going to let the rapidly-approaching birth of her first child pass without doing something to mark the occasion. A girls' night in was the plan. Initially, Nell planned to hold it at The Ducklings, since she did most of the cooking and it would be easier that way, but when Connor decided to take Gracie to visit his mother in Sheffield one Saturday, returning on the Sunday, the plan was changed to eating at Chestnut House. Anna's home was much larger than The Ducklings, and it would save her walking, or rather waddling, through the village to attend.

It had been a damp, dull sort of day, and Izzy was looking forward to getting out of Rose Cottage and catching up with her friends. She seemed to be immersed in the activities at Bramblewick Primary lately and needed to think about something else for a change.

Chestnut House felt wonderfully warm and welcoming when Rachel opened the door and ushered her inside. 'Come in. Isn't it awful out there? So miserable. I hate this time of year. Autumn is so depressing.'

'You're just missing Xander,' Izzy said, feeling sympathetic.

'No, honestly, it's not that.' Rachel grinned as they entered the cosy living room. 'Well, not *just* that. Don't you find November a horrible month? All dead leaves and puddles and gloomy skies.'

Nell and Anna were sitting together on the sofa, flicking through what appeared to be a catalogue of baby clothes and accessories. Izzy thought, with some alarm, that if Anna got any bigger she might just pop.

'I couldn't agree more,' Nell said, looking up and nodding at Rachel. 'I can't wait for spring, personally.'

'But the colours of autumn are so beautiful,' Anna said. 'All those reds

and golds and oranges. Just stunning.'
She dabbed at her eyes and Izzy gaped
at her.

'Are you crying?'

'Of course not!' Anna put the catalogue on the coffee table and stuffed her
tissue back inside her sleeve. 'I'm fine.'

'Hormones,' Nell said, squeezing her
arm. 'You shed all the tears you want,
love.'

'Hot chocolate, tea or coffee?' Rachel
enquired, taking Izzy's coat and scarf
from her. 'I'm in charge of the kettle
tonight. Anna's not moving from that
sofa. Connor's orders.'

'Look at the size of my ankles,' Anna
wailed.

Izzy raised an eyebrow. 'Never mind
your ankles. Look at that stomach! How
many babies have you got stuffed inside
there? Are you growing a litter?'

'There's only one,' Anna protested.
'Don't be so mean.'

'I think you look absolutely beautiful,' Nell assured her. 'You're glowing,
Anna.'

'Like an orange space hopper,' Izzy added, giggling.

Anna didn't laugh, and Izzy's giggles died. Oops. It seemed her friend's sense of humour had fallen prey to hormones, too. 'Sorry,' she said. 'Nell's right. You look lovely. I'm only teasing.'

'I don't feel lovely,' Anna admitted. 'I feel enormous. And I can't get comfortable, either. It's really hard to sleep. No one warned me about this stuff.'

'Be fair. If others warned us how awful pregnancy and childbirth were, no woman would go for it and the human race would die out,' Rachel said grimly. 'Izzy, what did you want to drink?'

'Oh, yeah, sorry. Er, coffee please.'

Izzy sank into the chair near the fireplace and shivered, holding out her hands to warm in front of the wood burner. 'So, how's maternity leave going?' she said. 'Are you still missing work?'

Anna sighed. 'I am, I suppose. Especially at the moment. Connor and

Riley are interviewing candidates for the new GP post. I'd love to have met them and given some input. I really hope they choose wisely.'

'We could do with a female GP,' Nell mused. 'That would be great.'

'I think there are a couple of female applicants,' Anna said, 'but they'll only go by qualifications, experience and personality. It's important that the new doctor fits in, and that they understand the way a small country practice works.'

'Like Connor did when he started here,' Izzy said, grinning.

'Bless him, he really did struggle, didn't he?' Anna leaned back on the sofa and closed her eyes, as if remembering. 'I really didn't think he'd settle, you know.'

'And look how that turned out!' Izzy let out a peal of laughter and Anna's eyes flew open.

'Are you just going to mock me all evening?'

Her tone was sharp, and Izzy's eyes widened. 'I wasn't mocking you, Anna. Far from it!'

Anna reached for her tissue again and Izzy sighed inwardly. She'd better be on her best behaviour, that much was clear. Her friend was obviously feeling super-sensitive right now.

It was with some relief that, upon hearing a knock on the front door, she hurried into the hallway to get away from Anna's reproachful stare. Her face broke into a wide smile as she threw open the door and found Holly standing on the step.

'Holls! You made it!'

She almost dragged her startled friend into the hallway and immediately began to take off her coat. 'Tea, coffee, hot chocolate?'

Holly rolled her eyes. 'Heck, Izzy, give me a chance! What's with the hot drinks, anyway? No alcoholic options?'

Izzy murmured, 'Solidarity with the pregnant lady.'

Holly pulled a face. 'Good job I brought this then.' She reached towards the coat that Izzy was now holding and rummaged in the pocket, withdrawing a small bottle of whisky. 'We can put a tot of that in our coffee,' she whispered. 'Anna need never know.'

'What need I never know?'

Izzy groaned inwardly on hearing Anna's voice. She turned, to see Anna standing at the foot of the stairs, eyeing them suspiciously.

Holly waved the bottle with no trace of guilt evident in her face. 'Whisky, Anna! Brought it to warm us up a bit. We weren't going to say anything because we didn't want you to feel left out, that's all.'

'I see.' Anna shrugged. 'No need to keep it a secret. I don't mind you drinking alcohol.' She wrinkled her nose. 'Sorry, Holls, got to go. Need the loo every five minutes these days. Make yourself at home.' She began to lumber up the stairs and Holly and Izzy wandered through to the living room where they were joined, within a minute or so, by Rachel, carrying a tray of drinks.

'Heard you come in,' she told Holly

cheerfully. 'Coffee okay?'

'More than okay,' Holly confirmed. 'I've brought this to add to the festivities,' she added, showing her the bottle.

'That's not really fair, is it?' Nell said, looking anxiously towards the door. 'I mean, Anna can't drink.'

'Anna said it's okay,' Holly assured her. 'It's just a tot in our coffee, Nell.'

Nell shook her head. 'I don't think we should. Anna's very emotional at the moment. You should have seen her blubbing this afternoon in Helmston.'

Izzy frowned. 'What were you doing in Helmston?'

Nell's face lit up. 'Shopping for a pram! Oh, you should see the one she's ordered. I can't say any more than that because it's up to Anna, but it's just gorgeous.'

Izzy felt a heavy weight in her chest. 'You went pram shopping with Anna?'

Nell nodded. 'Yeah. She asked me to go with her the other day. I don't think we could have left it any later, to be honest. She was worn out within an hour. The town was ever so busy and it was really cold, and it's only going to get worse as Christmas approaches. I think major shopping trips are best avoided until after she's had the baby.'

Anna entered the room, her eyes lighting up as she saw the mug of hot chocolate that Rachel had made her. 'Ooh, lovely. Thanks so much, Rachel.' She sat down heavily and reached for the mug. 'Mind you, if I drink this I'll be heading back to the bathroom in ten minutes.' She looked around at everyone. 'What are we talking about?'

'You,' Izzy said flatly. 'Going pram shopping with Nell this afternoon.'

'Oh.' Anna took a sip of her hot chocolate.

'I was just telling them how gorgeous the pram is,' Nell said. 'I didn't tell them any details, though. I know you want to show them the picture.'

Holly waved the bottle of whisky in the air with her usual lack of tact. 'Before you do that, anyone want a drop adding to their drink?'

Rachel shook her head. 'Not me. I'm driving.'

'More for the rest of us then.' Izzy held out her mug and Holly poured some of the fiery liquid into it, then offered the bottle to Nell.

Nell glanced at Anna and Izzy's stomach tightened as she said, after a moment's hesitation, 'No, it's okay. I'll not bother.'

Izzy couldn't hide her irritation as she snapped, 'Don't be such a misery. It's only a drop.'

To Izzy's amazement, Anna said smoothly, 'I'd rather you didn't, Nell, if you don't mind. People get very silly when they've had whisky. It will be nice to have you and Rachel still talking sense at the end of the night.'

Nell looked deeply uncomfortable and flashed Izzy an apologetic glance, but Izzy was too wounded to respond. Anna was clearly having a dig at her for drinking. It was just a tot of whisky in a coffee! What was with this sudden flourishing friendship between Nell and Anna? As if she couldn't guess. Clearly, her admission to Anna that she didn't want children had changed things between them.

Anna, hormones raging and in full mother-to-be mode, had shunned her in favour of Nell, and Nell was obviously revelling in her newly-elevated status.

Izzy felt desperately hurt. Not long ago, Anna would have asked her to go pram shopping with her. Heck, she wouldn't have even asked. It would have just been assumed, and quite rightly. Izzy would have loved to go with her. She felt a dullness settle on her that fully matched the autumn gloom outside.

'I'll show you the pram I've ordered,' Anna said, reaching, with some difficulty, for the coffee table where the catalogue sat. Nell hurriedly grabbed the catalogue and handed it to her, earning a grateful smile from Anna and a disgusted glare from Izzy. What a creep Nell was turning into!

'I suppose,' Anna confessed, flicking

through the pages of the catalogue, 'I should really have gone for a smaller, more practical pram, but I just couldn't resist.' She paused, turned back a page and then handed it to Holly, who was sitting closest to her, apart from Nell. 'There you go. That one. Bottom right.'

Holly peered at the page and whistled. 'Wow! That's a royal carriage of a baby's pram, isn't it?'

Rachel stood up and had a good look at the item in question. 'That's absolutely gorgeous, Anna! It will be wonderful to push that around the village.'

No one made any attempt to pass the catalogue to Izzy and she could feel her irritation growing by the minute. 'Let's have a look then,' she said eventually, since no one seemed inclined to share with her the image of the spectacular pram that Anna had purchased.

Anna made no move to hand it to her, and it was left to Rachel to pass the catalogue across. Izzy fought the urge to throw it back and walk out. She felt excluded, somehow, and she knew it must be in her imagination because, surely, Anna wouldn't have told the others about their conversation. Or would she? Suddenly, Izzy wasn't so sure any more and she realised her hands were trembling as she stared at the photograph of a huge navy blue and white carriage pram that wouldn't have looked out of place being pushed around the gardens of Kensington Palace.

'Good grief! How much?' The words escaped her mouth before she could stop them, and she knew immediately that she'd said the wrong thing.

'It's an investment,' Anna snapped. 'That pram will last for years.'

'Yes, but how many kids are you planning to have? You'd need to fill a classroom to get your money's worth from this!' She hadn't meant to be so mean, but Anna's tone had tipped her over the edge. There was something going on here and Izzy didn't know how to handle it. All she knew was, she wished she'd never told Anna the truth about herself and Matt and the reason for their break-up. Everything was spoilt.

Anna looked desolate and Izzy longed to tell her how sorry she was, and that she didn't mean it, but somehow, the words wouldn't come. An awkward silence hung over the room.

Holly broke it, mercifully. 'So, where's the grub? I'm starving, and I need to eat before I go.'

'Go?' Rachel swung round to face her. 'You're going already?'

'Not till I've got some food down me I'm not,' Holly pointed out. 'But, yeah, I have to leave early.'

'Oh, what a shame,' Nell said. 'Why?'

'I'm meeting Jonathan,' Holly explained. 'We're going for a drink in The Fox and Hounds and I can't be too late. So are you going to dish up or what?'

Rachel laughed. 'Might have known you wouldn't miss out on the food, Holls. Bet you're going to eat at The Fox and Hounds, too, aren't you?'

Holly pulled a face. 'Couldn't get a reservation, so no. Have you cooked, Nell?'

Nell stood up. 'I've made all sorts of stuff,' she confessed. 'I might have got a bit carried away. Come and help me, someone?'

'I'll help,' Izzy said quickly. Anything, she thought, to get away from Anna's reproachful silence. It was amazing how much her friend could say without so much as opening her mouth. Izzy had never felt uncomfortable around her before. She wished, with all her heart, that she could turn the clock back and not breathe a word to her about Matt.

* * *

Anna was yawning and clearly ready for bed. Izzy had hung on, hoping to get a moment or two alone with her, so they could patch up their friendship which seemed, to her at least, to be dangling by a thread.

Holly had, as promised, already left

to meet Jonathan, and Riley, ever the gentleman, had come to escort Nell back to The Ducklings. He'd offered to escort Izzy at the same time, but she'd mumbled some excuse about staying to finish her drink and assured him she would be absolutely fine. He'd seemed reluctant to leave her to walk home alone, but then Rachel had piped up that she would be able to drop Izzy home when she went back to Folly Farm, so Riley and Nell had departed.

Izzy had hoped that Rachel would leave soon after, but she'd stayed put, seeming in no rush to return home. Izzy supposed she couldn't blame her. At this time of night, her mother and Sam would be asleep in bed, and it must be horrible going home, knowing your partner wouldn't be there. At least she didn't have the ghost of Matt hanging around Rose Cottage. He'd never got as far as moving in, after all.

By the time Rachel started to get her coat on, Anna was clearly exhausted and made no secret of the fact. Izzy knew there was no way she could avoid going home with Rachel so, admitting defeat, she collected her own coat and scarf.

'Thanks for a lovely evening,' Anna said.

Rachel smiled. 'Thanks for having us. Now, you get yourself to bed. I've loaded the dishwasher so all you have to do is switch it on, and that can wait until morning. The kitchen's all neat and tidy. Get some sleep, okay?'

'You're a star, Rachel,' Anna said gratefully.

Izzy felt a pang of guilt. She should have been helping Rachel and Nell, but she'd wanted to talk to Anna properly and had stayed in the living room instead. It had been a waste of time, anyway, since Holly had hogged the entire conversation, banging on about how wonderful Jonathan was, and how happy he made her, and by the time she'd left to meet him in Helmston Nell and Rachel had returned to the living room, all the work done.

'Goodnight, Anna,' she murmured, as Rachel stepped outside into the dark and cold.

'Goodnight, Izzy,' Anna replied. 'Night, Rachel.'

Rachel shivered. 'Hurry up, Izzy,' she said, her breath escaping as a swirl of mist in the dark night air. 'It's freezing out here. You're letting all the warmth out.'

Izzy sighed and followed her out, hearing the door of Chestnut House close behind her straight away.

The two of them hurried down the path towards the garden gate. Mercifully, Rachel's car was parked just in front of the house, so they didn't have far to walk.

Within a few minutes they were driving away from Chestnut House, heading up the main street to Rose Cottage.

'You all right, Izz?' Rachel asked. 'Only, you've definitely not been yourself tonight.'

'I'm not the only one, am I?' Izzy said bitterly. 'What was up with Anna? That room was full of tension, don't you think?'

Rachel looked surprised. 'Tension? Not really, no. She had a few weepy moments, but that's to be expected. Other than that, she was her usual self.'

Izzy frowned. She couldn't even say that Rachel had been too tipsy to notice since she hadn't had any alcohol, so she couldn't imagine how her friend had missed the cold atmosphere in that house. She bit her lip, wondering if she dared to ask the question that had been bothering her all evening.

'Rachel,' she ventured at last, 'did Anna say anything to you? About the reason me and Matt broke up, I mean?'

Rachel glanced at her, surprised. 'No. Not a word. Why?'

Izzy shrugged. 'Just wondering.'

They were already pulling up outside Rose Cottage. Rachel kept the engine running, probably to stay warm, but turned to face Izzy. 'What's up, Izzy? You seem really down.'

Izzy was beginning to wish she hadn't

said anything. She probably wouldn't have done if whisky hadn't loosened her tongue, she thought. Great. Now there'd be two of her friends turning against her.

Rachel's eyes were warm with sympathy. 'You don't have to tell me, you know. If you'd rather not, I mean. But if you want to talk, I'm always here.'

'We broke up because I don't want children,' Izzy burst out.

There was quiet for a moment then Rachel said slowly, 'Right. And?'

Izzy said bitterly, 'Isn't that enough?'

'Well, I can see why you and Matt would break up if you couldn't agree on such an important matter, but what's it got to do with Anna? Because, clearly, you seem to feel it's had an effect on her. And why would you assume she's told me about it?'

'She was really shocked when I told her,' Izzy admitted. 'She couldn't seem to understand that I meant it.'

Rachel's brow furrowed. 'She probably just surprised that she hadn't known about it sooner. You two have been friends for years, haven't you?'

'Since schooldays,' Izzy confirmed.

'Well, there you are then. I think she's probably just a bit taken aback that she hadn't realised that about you earlier, that's all. Anna's not a judgmental sort of person, is she?'

'I wouldn't have said so, until now.' Izzy gazed out of the window, staring at the front door of her cottage. It was all in darkness. She wished she'd left a lamp on when she left.

'If it's any consolation,' Rachel said, 'I totally understand what you're saying. I never wanted children either.'

'You didn't?' Izzy's head shot round and she stared at Rachel in amazement. 'But you're so good with Sam!'

Rachel laughed. 'What do you expect me to do with him? Keep him in a kennel? Of course I'm good with him. He's my son and I love him. I couldn't love him more if I tried. But that doesn't change the fact that he wasn't planned, and I'd never intended to have children. Neither,' she added grimly, 'had Grant. He wasn't best pleased about it, I can tell you.'

'I know,' Izzy said softly, remembering Rachel's outburst in the summer when she'd revealed the true horror of her marriage to her ex-husband. He certainly hadn't given her an easy time, and he'd made her pregnancy miserable. 'But I don't intend to have a baby just to prove that I can be a mother, after all.'

'Of course you shouldn't do that! That's not what I'm saying at all. Obviously, for me, once Sam arrived things changed. I was very lucky because I fell in love with him immediately. It might not have happened that way and then how miserable we'd both have been. If you don't want children, Izzy, then you should stick by that. Don't let anyone sway you.'

'What about now?' Izzy said, curious. 'You're such a good mum. Would you want another child with Xander?'

Rachel shook her head. 'Xander and

I have both agreed that we're more than happy with what we already have. We both have careers we love, we're keen on building up Folly Farm as soon as he finishes work on *Lord Curtis Investigates*, and we have Sam and all our animals. We don't need anything else.'

'You're very lucky that Xander feels that way,' Izzy mumbled. 'Matt certainly didn't.'

'I know. I realise that, honestly.' Rachel put her hand over Izzy's. 'But you shouldn't have a baby just because your partner wants one. You did absolutely the right thing telling Matt how you felt and working all that out before you moved in together. It would have been so much more painful further down the line. Not every man wants kids, Izzy, and I'm sure you'll find someone who feels the same as you do at some point.'

'I'll take your word for it,' Izzy said grimly. 'In the meantime, what do I do about Anna?'

Rachel let out a long breath. 'I wouldn't worry about Anna too much. I think you're reading too much into things. I honestly didn't notice any change in her attitude towards you. She was obviously tired and hormonal, but that's to be expected.'

'She didn't ask me to go pram shopping with her,' Izzy said, hating herself for sounding like a petulant child. 'We always did stuff like that together. When she was going to marry Lee, I was the one pushing her to organise the wedding. We shared a house for goodness sake! And we planned her wedding to Connor together, too. I can't believe she's pushed me out of this; the most important thing that's ever happened to her.'

Rachel shrugged. 'Maybe she just thought that it would be awkward for you, after you'd told her how you felt?'

'Or maybe she thought that, because I don't want a baby of my own, I wouldn't be in the slightest bit interested in hers!'

'Are you interested in hers?'

'Of course I am! Anna's my best friend. I love Gracie, don't I? Why on earth wouldn't I love her new baby?'

'Then why don't you just tell her that?' Rachel said gently. 'Anna's so maternal she's probably struggling to understand that someone who doesn't want kids could still be interested in, and loving towards, other people's. Just remind her of the fact.'

Izzy tutted. 'I shouldn't have to. It's obvious.'

'Well, it is to you, and to me, too, but Anna's in a fog at the moment. If you want to keep your friendship on track, isn't it worth making the effort?'

Izzy reached for her bag. 'Thanks for the lift, Rachel, and for listening. I appreciate it.'

'No worries. Chin up, Izzy. Things will look better in the morning,' Rachel assured her.

As Izzy hurried down the path towards her front door, she wished she could share Rachel's optimism. Hearing the car pull away, heading out of the village towards Folly Farm, she unlocked the door and practically fell inside, glad that, at least, she'd had the foresight to keep the central heating on. There'd been enough coldness to deal with that night. Whatever Rachel said, she knew something was wrong with Anna, and it didn't take a genius to work out what that was. She wasn't sure things would ever be the same between them again.

★   ★   ★

Jackson handed Ash a bottle of Lusty Tup beer and sank into the armchair with a blissful sigh. 'Nothing better than a bottle of beer and a lazy Sunday in front of the telly,' he pronounced.

Ash raised an eyebrow. 'Lazy Sunday? You've spent all day so far cleaning this place. Look at it, it's immaculate!'

He gazed around the sparklingly clean room, thinking ruefully of the messy flat he'd left behind and wishing he'd tidied up before he left. Now he would have to face it all when he got back, and he wasn't sure he had the energy. 'If I give you a tenner, would you come round to my place and clean that for me?'

Jackson tutted. 'Lazy devil. I don't know how you can stand to live in a mess. It would drive me insane.'

'Clearly. There's such a thing as overdoing it, though, you know.' Ash took a swig from the beer bottle and smacked his lips together in appreciation. 'Good beer that.'

'I know. Let's make the most of what's left of today. Here's to Sundays. Back to the fray tomorrow.'

'Don't remind me,' Ash said, tipping his bottle towards Jackson's in a silent toast. 'So much to be getting on with. Can't believe we're almost into December now.'

'How's the play coming along?' Jackson queried. 'Have you got all the principal parts cast?'

'Mostly. We're still debating a couple, but we kind of know what we want. We've sent out letters of consent to all the parents, and we've got some of the TAs on board. They're going to help out with painting the backdrops, and with props. We're putting out a plea for donations for bedding, old clothes, that kind of thing. Tomorrow, we're figuring out where to slot the carols into scenes from the play, so we can include more of the children. Are you still up for playing the piano for the carols, by the way?'

Jackson nodded. 'Told you I would. At least that's not too taxing, although rehearsals are going to be a pain.' He considered the matter. 'It shouldn't be too difficult to fit carols into that play, anyway. You've got a whole bunch of little orphan children who can burst into song at any moment.'

'There's already a soundtrack to the play, remember,' Ash said. 'We've got to make it look natural, not shoehorned in.'

'What about costumes? The dressing-up box isn't exactly overflowing.'

'We're going to ask parents to dig out

any old clothes that the children don't wear anymore and shred them up a bit, so they look raggy and worn for the orphans. The ghosts shouldn't be too taxing. We thought a simple party dress and maybe a tinsel headband for the Ghost of Christmas Past, and a dressing gown and holly wreath headband for Christmas Present. As for the Ghost of Christmas Yet to Come — some sort of hooded cape or robe should do the trick. I'm sure we'll come up with something.'

'And Scrooge?'

'We're going to have a look through the dressing-up box and see what we can make from it. There's plenty of time for now. The main thing is to get all the consent forms back and get our cast in place.'

'Do you ever wish you hadn't bothered?' Jackson stroked his dark beard thoughtfully. 'You could have got away with it this year, you know. It was your one chance and you blew it.'

Ash took another sip of beer. 'I

couldn't just leave Izzy to flounder. She didn't have a clue what she was doing.'

Jackson gave him a sly grin. 'You always did have a soft spot for her,' he remarked.

'I did not!' Ash spluttered.

'Yes, you did!' Jackson said nothing for a moment, then ventured, 'Remember Skimmerdale?'

Ash could feel the heat searing through his cheeks. He was sort of hoping Jackson had forgotten all about that. 'That was ages ago.'

'A couple of years.' Jackson reached for the remote control. 'Quite an adventure, wasn't it?'

Ash didn't reply. He was remembering the week that he and a small group of his colleagues had taken some of the children to stay in a hostel on the outskirts of a pretty Yorkshire Dales market town, Kirkby Skimmer. School trips weren't generally his thing, but one of his fellow teachers had dropped out at the last moment, due to illness, and Mrs Morgan had been desperate for a replacement. He hadn't been looking forward to it, but it had turned out to be an enjoyable week, exploring the pretty Dales villages, studying the geology and geography of the area, the history of the Cistercian abbey in the town, and . . . other things.

'I honestly thought something would have come from that, you know,' Jackson mused. 'You seemed so well suited, and there was certainly something sizzling away that night we got home and celebrated.'

'Oh, shut up!' Ash rolled his eyes. 'Are you actually going to use that remote control or is it just for decoration?'

Jackson grinned. 'Point taken. Now, *Die Hard* or *Home Alone*?'

Ash pulled a face. 'What do you think?'

'Quite right,' Jackson said, nodding. '*Home Alone* it is then.'

5

Izzy had intended to go straight home from work. It was dark, cold and miserable outside, and she couldn't wait to get into her pyjamas, snuggle down in front of the fire and watch her favourite soap before the usual round of evening marking. When she saw the Christmas lights twinkling in the window of Spill the Beans, the local cafe and bakery, though, she changed her mind. Rather than go back to Rose Cottage and start cooking, she decided she'd treat herself to something ready-made. She might as well sit in a warm, cosy cafe and eat, then she could go home without having to start cooking.

Nell and her assistant, Chloe, were both behind the counter when she walked in. For a brief moment, Izzy closed her eyes, breathing in the blissful fragrance of warm pastries and freshly-brewed coffee, and revelling in the warmth that wrapped around her like a duvet, so welcome after the icy air outside.

'Didn't expect to see you tonight,' Nell said, her cheerful tones cutting through Izzy's moment of tranquil joy and making her open her eyes once more. 'You don't usually come in here on a week day.'

'I really haven't got the energy to cook,' Izzy confessed. 'I know you'll be closing in half an hour, but can I get something to eat?'

'To eat in or take away, do you mean?'

'Eat in. I just want to sit down, get warm, and be fed for a change. I can't face standing in the kitchen making something from scratch, and I haven't got any ready meals in the freezer.'

'Sit yourself down,' Nell said, smiling. 'Have a browse through the menu and give me a shout when you've decided what you want. In the meantime, cup of coffee?'

'Oh, please,' Izzy said gratefully.

She made her way to the table nearest the radiator and leaned back in her chair, glad to be warm again.

After perusing the menu, she decided on a simple sausage and baked bean pasty with chips and relayed her decision to Nell when she delivered the coffee.

'Coming right up,' Nell promised.

She was as good as her word. Fifteen minutes later, Izzy was tucking into a delicious pasty and feeling a lot more cheerful than she had in days. She glanced around the cafe, smiling to herself at the pretty fairy lights and Christmas tree. Spill the Beans was always one of the first places in the village to be decorated for the festive season. Nell was such a romantic, and she loved Christmas. Being here, Izzy began to feel a lot more festive herself, which was a pleasant change. She'd begun to think that the stresses and strains of organising the Christmas play were enough to put her off for life.

Eventually, Izzy was the only person

left in the cafe, apart from Nell. Even Chloe had disappeared into the kitchen. Things were definitely winding down for the evening, she thought, gulping down the last of her coffee before Nell decided to throw her out.

'Aw, thanks, Izzy. You didn't have to do that,' Nell said when Izzy brought her empty cup and plate to the counter.

'I can see you're itching to clean up and close and I don't blame you. Can't wait to get home and get cosied up in front of the telly myself,' Izzy confessed. 'How's it going with Riley? Not cramping your style yet?'

Nell's smile told her all she needed to know. Clearly, things were going very well indeed. 'He's just lovely,' Nell said, sounding almost shy. 'Things really couldn't be better.'

'That's great,' Izzy said, trying not to feel jealous. It wasn't Nell's fault that Anna had asked her to go pram shopping with her, after all, and she was a good person, as was Riley. They deserved their happiness.

'How's it going with the play?' Nell enquired.

'Things are on track,' Izzy said warily.

'Anna said Gracie's got the role of Ghost of Christmas Past,' Nell said, her eyes shining. 'I'll bet she'll be wonderful in that part. Anna's very relieved that Gracie's got something to focus on at last. She's been a bit worried about her lately, hasn't she?'

Izzy felt a surge of irritation and a pathetic wave of jealousy. 'I don't know. Has she?'

'Well, yeah. She's been a bit temperamental these last few days, and she keeps going on about getting a dog, and she's not showing any interest in the baby. Anna's quite worried, and so is Connor. This play will give her something to occupy her and they're hoping she'll start to settle down again.'

'Right.' Once upon a time, Izzy thought wretchedly, she'd be the person who knew that, not Nell. She felt angry with Anna for confiding in their friend instead of in her; in Nell for being the one Anna seemed to be turning to and, most of all, in herself for being pathetic enough to care so much. 'Well, let's hope it works then. I've got to go, Nell. Got a stack of marking to get through tonight.'

'And I've got to clean up here and get home in time to make Riley's tea,' Nell said, smiling. 'He leaves surgery at six.'

'How sexist,' Izzy said, feeling mean but seeming unable to stop herself.

Nell looked rather surprised. 'Not at all. He does more than his fair share around the house. Just that, I get home first and I love to cook, so why not?'

'Why not indeed?'

'Are you okay, Izzy?' Nell said, frowning. 'You don't seem your usual self.'

'I'm absolutely fine,' Izzy assured her, buttoning up her coat and winding her scarf around her neck. 'Thanks for the meal, Nell. It was delicious. See you later.'

'Bye, Izz.'

Nell still looked puzzled as Izzy opened the door and stepped outside into the street. The blast of icy air hit her in the face and she shivered, feeling almost as cold on the inside. She'd never considered herself a jealous person before but being pushed out of Anna's life was hurting her like she'd never imagined it could. She simply had to get a grip.

★   ★   ★

Izzy was exhausted. It had been a frantic week at the school. Apart from the usual workload — as if that wasn't always heavy enough — she and Caroline had been getting the children to make Christmas decorations to adorn the classroom, as well as working on the fast-approaching Christmas play.

Caroline had been left in charge of the class while Izzy spent the afternoon in the hall, going over key scenes with leading cast members.

A young boy called Benjy Adams had

been given the part of Ebenezer Scrooge, and he was clearly relishing the chance to show off his acting skills, wringing his hands and scowling like a proper pantomime villain.

'Someone's been watching *A Christmas Carol* on a loop,' Ash murmured as he and Izzy stood by the stage, watching in awe as Benjy heaped misery on poor Sara Coombes, the nine-year-old who was playing widowed Mrs Cratchitt, housekeeper at the orphanage owned by Ebenezer. A couple of the TAs were in the hall and they were obviously impressed, too, judging by their encouraging smiles and nods.

'Isn't she doing well?' Izzy said, smiling as Sara begged and pleaded with Scrooge for extra helpings of gruel for the orphans. 'Such a shy girl usually, too. This is really bringing her out of her shell.'

'This is what I love about the school plays,' Ash told her. 'You get to see a whole different side to the children. The boisterous kids seem to calm down and concentrate more, and the shy kids bloom. It's such a fantastic thing to see.'

Izzy saw the light in his hazel eyes and heard the enthusiasm in his tone. She couldn't help but smile, her heart lifting at his obvious joy. It was infectious. No wonder he volunteered for the job every year.

Suddenly, she noticed his expression change. His face took on an anxious look and he murmured, 'Uh oh.' Following his gaze, she saw Gracie, standing in the corner of the hall, her arms wrapped around herself as she rocked back and forth, looking deeply agitated.

Ash was already on his way over to her, and Izzy followed, her own anxiety growing.

'Gracie.' Ash bent down and looked Gracie in the eye. For a moment, she didn't seem to even notice he was there, but as he repeated her name she stared at him, a frightened look on her face. 'Let's go and sit in the staff room, shall we? Nice and quiet in there. We can get some peace.'

Izzy held her breath, then let it out slowly as Gracie nodded dumbly and followed Ash out of the hall. She cast a nervous look at the stage, but the TAs knew what was supposed to be happening in this rehearsal, so she decided to leave them to it for a short while and make sure Gracie was okay. Ash might need her help if she had a complete meltdown. It had happened before, after all. Hopefully, he'd spotted the warning signs in time and would be able to head it off.

The staff room was empty apart from Ash and Gracie. Neither glanced up as she entered the room, but she knew that Ash, at least, was aware she was there. Gracie was now still and silent, sitting in one of the comfortable chairs as Ash spoke to her calmly and quietly. Izzy sat down next to him and listened as he asked Gracie if she wanted to talk.

Gracie didn't reply. Her hands

gripped the wooden arms of the chair as she stared at the wall opposite.

Ash reached into his pocket and took out his phone. Izzy watched as he tapped it a few times, then she leaned back in the chair as soft music began to fill the air. Ash put the phone on the occasional table nearby and leaned back in his own chair, looking relaxed. After a few moments, Gracie's posture seemed to loosen up. She exhaled deeply, as if she'd been holding her breath, then she, too, leaned back in her chair and closed her eyes.

For a few minutes the three of them sat there, saying nothing, simply listening to the gentle music in the background. Izzy glanced at her watch, wondering if she should get back to rehearsals and leave Ash and Gracie to it. Ash certainly seemed to have everything under control. Gracie had been in real danger of having one of her meltdowns, but Ash seemed to have averted it.

She watched him as he sat calmly, his manner so assured and reassuring that she couldn't imagine anyone losing control around him. Well, not in that sort of way anyway . . . She blinked, realising which way her train of thought was running. Good grief, where had that come from? She'd better get back to the hall and immerse herself in a different type of fantasy altogether.

'Why do people keep asking me if I'm excited about the baby?' Gracie's voice cut through the quiet, and Izzy snapped to attention.

Ash seemed to consider for a moment. '*Do* people keep asking you that?'

'Yes they do. All the time.'

Ash said gently, 'I expect they're just being polite.'

'But it's a stupid question,' Gracie protested. 'Why would I be excited about the baby? I haven't met it yet. How do I know if it's a good thing or a bad thing?'

Ash rubbed his chin. 'Good point.'

'It's all anyone talks about,' Gracie muttered.

'Well, if anyone asks again, just tell

them what you've told us,' Ash said reasonably.

'I wish we were getting a dog instead of a baby,' Gracie told him.

Izzy glanced at Ash. He raised his eyebrows and she shook her head slightly. 'Maybe,' she said, 'one day you will get a dog. Just not yet. It's the wrong time for it, because you've got such a lot going on already.'

'That's what Dad and Anna say,' Gracie said. 'But I don't see why. Babies don't take up much room and they'll be looking after it anyway. I'd be looking after the puppy.'

'Puppies,' Izzy pointed out, 'are babies too, and two babies in a house at the same time would be a lot to deal with. And don't forget, Gracie, that it's Christmas soon. The house will be very busy, and a puppy would get in the way.'

'You know sometimes,' Ash said, 'when there's a lot of noise, or bright lights, and you get upset with yourself and can't cope with it all?'

Gracie nodded suspiciously. 'What about it?'

'Well, that's how a puppy would feel if you took it home to Chestnut House when there's a new baby around and a Christmas tree and fairy lights. Imagine all that noise, with a baby crying, and then the tree lights and the fire crackling and the wrapping paper making that scrunching noise when you open your presents. A puppy wouldn't like that at all.'

'Which is why it's best to wait until the baby's a bit bigger and Christmas is over,' Izzy finished. 'You're ten now, and you've learned how to cope with a lot of this stuff, but a puppy just couldn't handle it. Do you see that?'

Gracie seemed to consider the matter for a while, then she nodded reluctantly. 'I suppose so. But I really do want a dog.'

'Maybe,' said Ash, 'you could spend the time while you're waiting for a puppy productively.'

'What do you mean?' Gracie looked

puzzled. 'Can you turn that music off now, please?' she added, putting her hands to her ears.

Ash switched off his phone and faced Gracie, his expression earnest. 'You've got a great opportunity now to do some research. Find out all about the different breeds of dog. Make a checklist. Work out which type would suit you and your family best. Go online and print off some information. Go to the school library and look for some books about dog care. Learn how to look after them properly, and about training them. By the time you get your puppy, you'll know exactly how to look after him, and then he'll be the best-loved and most well looked-after puppy in Bramblewick.'

Gracie looked delighted. 'I could do that, couldn't I?'

'Certainly you could.' Ash smiled at her. 'Is it a plan?'

'Oh, yes. I think so,' Gracie acknowledged. She settled back, looking much happier. 'Should I go back to rehearsals now?'

Ash glanced at Izzy.

'Shall we leave rehearsals for today?' Izzy suggested. 'How about Mr Uttridge goes back to the hall and I stay here with you for a while, until you feel like going back to class? We can do some rehearsals tomorrow instead.'

Gracie hesitated a moment, then nodded. 'Can I have the music back on for a while then please?'

Ash handed the phone to Izzy. 'I'll collect it after rehearsals are finished,' he told her. As he put the mobile into her hand he whispered, 'Come and get me if you need me.'

She nodded, watching him closely as he walked out of the staff room.

Gracie gave a big sigh. 'I like Mr Uttridge, don't you?'

'I do,' Izzy said softly. 'I really do.'

6

Izzy's class was busy making decorations for the Christmas tree in the hall when she left the classroom, heading to rehearsals for *A Twisted Christmas*. Excitement was high among the children. A small Christmas tree now stood on top of the corner bookshelf, and various paper decorations had been created by the children to adorn the classroom. For the past few days, the room had been awash with glitter, tinsel, glue, card and tissue paper.

Unfortunately for Izzy, because rehearsals had to be fitted in around the all-important maths and English lessons, she found that she was missing a lot of the creative lessons with her class and having to leave the children with Caroline. She felt quite glum about that, as she loved this time of year when the kids' faces were bright with excitement and joy.

Every morning now, the post box in the hall was emptied and deliveries were made to each class, as the children posted their Christmas cards to their friends and teachers. Izzy had written on all her cards and planned to post them within the next day or two. Every single child in her class would receive one from her, and she'd budgeted to get them all a small selection box to open, too.

The hall was a welcoming room at this time of year. A high-ceilinged, often cold-looking space, it was now adorned with a multitude of Christmas cards, festive paintings, paper decorations and tinsel. The large Christmas tree in the corner was still fairly bare, but the kids were working on rectifying the situation at that very moment. Before long, it would be packed to the brim with the paper chains, cardboard Santas, and glitter-sprinkled angels that the children had created. December was going by fast and Christmas was creeping ever closer, along with the play.

Ash was already going through the rehearsal plan with the children when Izzy walked in. Gracie wasn't present. They had agreed that she would only be called from her classroom when she was due to go on stage, as the waiting around unsettled her too much.

'My fault entirely,' Ash had confessed. 'I knew that from last year, but I got distracted. Gracie can't be left waiting like that. She has too much time to worry and overthink. I feel really bad for what happened.'

'You shouldn't,' Izzy had assured him. 'You handled the situation beautifully and really calmed her down. I can't believe you coped so well.'

He smiled. 'I've had over a year learning her triggers and how to defuse her meltdowns, remember. Distraction's usually the best way with Gracie. Music calms her most of the time. Then the dog situation really helped, because it gave her something else to think about.'

'It was inspired!' Izzy said, admiringly. 'Anna and Connor really do want to get her a dog because they know how much she's always liked Jacko — he's the Twidales' sheepdog — but the timing's really not right just yet. Your suggestions will occupy her until they feel able to buy her a puppy.'

'And you know how obsessed she gets with things,' Ash agreed. 'She'll know everything there is to know about dogs before too long, and she'll be able to judge which breed is the right one for that family. Hopefully that will hold her off for a while.'

'Anna and Connor owe you a huge debt,' Izzy told him.

He laughed. 'Well, I wouldn't go that far, but if I can help at all it's a good thing. They have a lot to deal with. I really admire them, especially now they've got a new baby on the way, too. That's a lot to take on for anyone, but with Gracie to handle, on top of that . . .'

'I'm sure they're up to it,' Izzy murmured.

He nodded. 'No doubt. They're very good parents.'

'Yeah, they are.' Izzy had felt uncomfortable suddenly. She didn't want to get onto the whole subject of parenting with Ash. If anyone was a born father, it was him. He was so good with children, she could see him at home surrounded by at least half a dozen of his own. Best not to dwell on it.

'How's it going?' she asked now, as she headed towards the stage where Ash was standing, issuing directions to Abel Thomas, who was playing The Ghost of Christmas Yet to Come. Abel was relishing the role, being extremely dramatic as he pointed accusingly at Ebenezer Scrooge and promised a fate too fearful to contemplate.

'Great,' Ash confirmed. 'We've had lots of costumes coming in from the parents. Most of the orphans are kitted out now, and the dressing-up box is getting nicely topped up.' His face brightened. 'Guess what Dawn found in a charity shop in York the other day?'

'What?'

'A top hat! An actual top hat! Perfect for our Artful Dodger, don't you think?'

Izzy smiled. 'Perfect.'

'I couldn't believe it when she brought it in for me,' he admitted. 'I could have hugged her.'

Izzy felt a most peculiar sensation in her stomach, as it seemed to flip over in response to his words. What on earth was that? Surely — surely, she wasn't jealous? Ridiculous! 'That's great. I was thinking that we need to go over the reception class's Christmas carol a few times. Time's ticking on. Would Jackson be available tomorrow, do you think?'

Ash shrugged. 'I'll ask him at break. I've been thinking that we should work on a proper schedule together so that we know exactly how much time we've got for each section of the play, and the other teachers and TAs know where they are. What do you think?'

'I think that's a great idea,' Izzy said.

Ash clapped his hand to his forehead.

'I'm sorry, Izzy. I've taken over, haven't I? This is your call. You're in charge. I forget sometimes, I'm so used to doing all this myself. We'll do it your way.'

Izzy grinned. 'But your way is so much better, and you're right. I should have organised something more structured myself. How about we work on it later today?'

Ash considered. 'Tell you what, why don't you come round to my flat for dinner tonight? We'll have something to eat and then we can go over the whole thing, scene by scene, and draw up a rota for all the teachers and TAs involved. I've got a printer at home, so we can print off copies for everyone. What do you think?'

Izzy couldn't deny the thrill she felt at the thought of spending the evening with Ash, but that worried her. She shouldn't be feeling like this. He was her colleague, and hadn't she been the one who'd told Anna that work and play didn't mix? Besides, Ash wasn't her type, and she doubted very much that he was hers. He'd go for someone much more housewifely, she thought. A real maternal type . . .

He was watching her, a hopeful look in his eyes. She saw the gold flecks around the hazel-coloured irises, and noticed that he had rather thick, black eyelashes. He had kind eyes, she thought. Gentle eyes. He was a gentleman in every sense of the word. She was lost.

'I think that's a great idea,' she said, vowing to herself that tonight would be all about the Christmas play, and she would keep all her silly fancies and romantic notions firmly in check.

*　*　*

'Don't tell me,' Izzy said, as she entered Ash's flat and sniffed the air appreciatively. 'Spaghetti Bolognese!'

'Why would you say that?' Ash said, looking puzzled.

'Men always seem to cook that,' she told him. 'It's as if it's the only thing they ever learn how to do.'

'Well, for your information, it's not spaghetti Bolognese,' Ash said haughtily. 'It's lasagne.'

Izzy held up her hands. 'Okay, it's lasagne. Fair enough. Whatever it is, it smells delicious and I've just realised how hungry I am.'

'Should be ready in about half an hour,' Ash told her. 'Here, let me take your coat. The kettle's on.'

Izzy handed him her coat, glancing around the living room of his flat as she did so. It was a big room, and he had some nice furniture in there. She loved the old dresser that sat against one wall, packed to the brim with old, mismatched china. He had plenty of bookshelves, too, which was always a good sign. She sank down into his distressed chestnut leather sofa. She loved his taste in furniture; she just wasn't too sure about the flat. It was in a modern building and the place had no character, as much as he'd tried to give it some. It had low skirting boards, and there were no cornices or coving, no alcoves or interesting nooks, or quirks of any kind.

Ash came through from the kitchen, carrying a tray with two mugs of tea on it. 'What do you think?' he said, nodding round at the flat. 'Do you like my fire? Beats your genuine, wood burning stove any day of the week, doesn't it?'

Izzy looked at the electric stove sitting on a modern fireplace and tried to think of a tactful reply. 'I'm sure it's much more convenient,' she said carefully, hoping that would satisfy him.

Ash burst out laughing. 'It's okay, Izzy, you don't have to be kind. I know it's awful. My attempt to inject some character into a building that doesn't even have a proper chimney. It's a horrible flat, but it's big and it's fairly cheap, and it was all I could find at the time, so . . . '

Izzy felt relieved. 'It's certainly big,' she agreed. 'Makes my little cottage look like a shoebox.'

'Oh, but your place is perfect,' he said immediately, clearly meaning it. 'My absolute dream home. All those old beams, and the whitewashed walls and that huge fireplace! You're so lucky to have found it.'

Izzy was quite flattered. She loved Rose Cottage and it was gratifying to discover that he loved it, too. 'I didn't really find it,' she admitted. 'It was my parents' home. I grew up there.'

'Really?' Ash sounded surprised.

'Yes, really. I don't think I fully appreciated it at the time, though. It only has two bedrooms, and the second one is tiny. I used to grumble about it all the time when I was a kid, and I wanted them to move to a new house, can you believe? It was only when I went to university and stayed in various student houses and flats that I began to miss the character of home. When Mum and Dad decided to retire to Spain, they signed it over to me. They wanted it to remain in the family and they refused to take a penny from me.

Let's face it, with my job I could never have afforded to pay them what it's worth.'

'That was really good of them,' Ash agreed.

'It was. I did protest, but they wouldn't budge. Their reasoning was that they'd have left it to me in their will, anyway, so in their eyes it was already mine. They'd been considering renting it out if I hadn't got the job back in Bramblewick, and they were delighted that I wanted to live in it. It worked out well for all of us.'

'Are they happy in Spain?' Ash asked, lifting the mug of tea to his lips.

'Love it,' Izzy confirmed. She pulled a face as her stomach rumbled loudly. 'Gosh, I'm sorry! Did you hear that? I didn't have any lunch, I'm afraid. I'm starving.'

'I hope my lasagne fills you up then,' he said, laughing. 'I'll just go and see how it's doing.'

The lasagne did fill her up. Izzy couldn't believe how tasty it was. 'You really made this all yourself?'

'I really did,' he promised. 'With the help of dried lasagne sheets, some mince and two jars of pasta sauce.'

'I knew it!' Izzy giggled. 'Still, who cares as long as it tastes good?'

'My thoughts exactly.' Ash grinned at her. 'Now, shall I make us a hot drink, or would you like some wine?'

'Tea would be fine,' Izzy said. 'We've got work to do, remember?'

'You're quite right,' he agreed, heading into the kitchen to make the tea.

It took a good couple of hours to come up with the rota for rehearsals. Having to work out which children were in which scene, figure out which of their TAs were involved, when teachers would be free, and when each child would be needed in class for essential lessons was a time-consuming and headache-inducing task. They used pencils and paper to start with, making rough plans and erasing them again as new thoughts and problems occurred to them. When they finally knew what they were doing, Izzy typed up the lot on Ash's computer and he printed them off, making sure there was a rota for each classroom, so all children, teachers and TAs knew what they were doing and when.

Finally, exhausted, they sank onto the sofa and stared at each other. 'We did it.'

Izzy rubbed her eyes. 'What a mammoth task that was!' Her mouth curved upwards as excitement took hold. 'It's really taking shape, though, isn't it?'

'It is,' Ash agreed. 'The kids are doing so well, and they're really enjoying it.' He hesitated. 'Would you like that glass of wine now?'

Izzy looked at her watch and pulled a face. 'I really ought to be getting home,' she said reluctantly. 'Back to the coal face tomorrow morning, after all.'

He looked disheartened. 'Yeah, right. Of course.'

Izzy rolled her eyes. 'Oh, go on then!

You've twisted my arm. Just one, mind, and a small one, at that. I *am* driving, remember!'

'Absolutely.'

Ash was as good as his word, returning with a glass of white wine that was no bigger than a single pub measure. He handed it to her and sat down beside her, raising his own glass to hers. 'To a job well done.'

'I'll drink to that,' she agreed, clinking her glass against his.

Two hours later, they'd gone through a whole bottle of wine and Izzy was well-resigned to having to call for a taxi to take her home.

'I can't believe how weak-willed I am,' she admitted. 'I suppose it's the relief that we've managed to plan a rota and that the play's coming on so well. I was ever so worried. I can't think what possessed me to take it on.'

'It looked to me,' Ash said carefully, 'as if you were trying to distract yourself from something. Or someone.'

Izzy's laughter died, and she stared

into her wine glass. 'This is almost empty,' she said. 'Got any more?'

Ash shook his head. 'Funnily enough, I don't have a wine cellar, I'm afraid. That was the only bottle I had in and I think it's been there since last Christmas. I might have the odd bottle of Lusty Tup beer in my fridge if you fancy a change?'

'Lusty Tup!' Izzy decided that would be a big mistake. 'No thanks. Who knows what effect that might have?'

'Well, yeah.' Ash stared at her and she stared back, suddenly feeling terribly hot.

'So,' Ash cleared his throat and made an obvious effort to sound brisk and business-like, 'were you working to forget?'

'Working to forget?' Izzy feigned ignorance but he clearly wasn't fooled.

'Volunteering for the school play. Not something that's ever seemed to appeal to you before. I was wondering why now, and the only thing I can come up with is what you told me that first day.'

129

Izzy's brow furrowed. 'What did I tell you?'

Ash tilted his head to one side, his expression sympathetic. 'That you were single. I know for a fact that you've been dating Matt Jones for months, so that came as quite a surprise.'

Izzy's mouth fell open. He wasn't the only one that was surprised. 'How did you know that?' she demanded.

'That you were dating Matt?' He shrugged. 'It's a small village, Izz.'

Something about the way he said her name made her shiver. He was right, it was a small village, but she hadn't realised he'd even been aware that she existed outside of the school gates, never mind knew who she was dating. 'Well, yeah, I was seeing him for a few months,' she said cautiously. 'It didn't work out.'

'I'm sorry.'

'Are you?' Why on earth had she said that, and in that sort of tone! The tone that said, *are you really, or are you actually glad to know that I'm back on*

130

the market? As if he'd care, one way or the other!

'It's hard when relationships end,' he said.

'It is,' she acknowledged. 'Have to say, it wasn't one of my finest moments. He'd just agreed to move in with me and then it was all over before he could even pack a case. How embarrassing is that?'

Ash shrugged. 'You want embarrassing? What about me? I was engaged to someone once, you know.'

'You were?' Izzy was surprised, having never heard so much as a whisper about Ash's private life.

'Yeah, before I moved to Bramblewick.' His eyes twinkled, and his mouth twitched. 'It was a long engagement.'

'Really? How long?'

'Seven hours. Longest seven hours of my life.' He threw back his head and laughed and, after a moment's astonished silence, Izzy joined him.

'Crikey, seven hours! That makes me feel much better.'

'Cos you're not the biggest loser in the room?'

'Aw, don't say that. You're not a loser, and neither am I.' She sighed. 'At least, I hope not.'

'You're not a loser, Izzy,' he said. He took her hand and squeezed it gently. 'Far from it.'

Izzy gulped. 'Well, you would say that. You don't want me to fire you.'

He grinned. 'There is that. But, anyway, I happen to know you're a great kisser.'

Izzy's face burned. 'How on earth would you know that?' Surely, Matt hadn't told anyone? He didn't even know Ash, did he? Unless, perish the thought, they had a mutual acquaintance. It was lovely to get a positive review, but she wasn't sure she liked the idea of her being the topic of conversation among her ex and his friends.

'Don't you remember?' His thumb stroked her hand. 'Seriously? I'm wounded.'

'You've lost me. What do you mean?'

Ash dropped her hand and held his own to his heart, rather dramatically. 'For shame! How forgettable was mine own kiss! Yet I wilst ne'er forget the taste of thine own sweet lips, fair maiden.'

Izzy folded her arms, feeling completely bewildered. 'Just how drunk are you?'

He tutted. 'God, you really don't remember, do you? Our kiss? Have to say, Izzy, I'm a bit embarrassed that I made such a feeble impression on you.'

'I've never kissed you! I mean, you never — we never . . . ' Izzy shook her head, stunned.

'Are you making this up?'

'Remember the school trip to that hostel in Kirkby Skimmer the other year?'

Of course she remembered. Five members of staff had taken over thirty pupils to the Yorkshire Dales for a week and it had been much more fun than she'd expected. On the last evening, she and Ash and a teaching assistant called

Dom had headed into town to a pretty little pub, The Monk's Haven, for a couple of beers. They'd enjoyed a great evening while their colleagues, Jackson and Deena, had been kind enough to stay at the hostel to make sure the children were okay. She remembered she and Ash had taken part in a pub quiz and they'd had a real laugh together, but that was all.

'I remember the trip, of course I do. But what's that got to do with anything?'

Ash narrowed his eyes. 'You've really forgotten, haven't you? Quite offended, here, Izzy.'

He sounded as if he was trying to make light of the issue, but deep down she could tell he was genuinely bothered that she'd apparently dismissed whatever had happened from her mind.

'When we got home and had handed the children back to their parents, we all went out for the evening to celebrate a job well done, remember? We went to Whitby on a pub crawl.' He pulled a face. 'Admittedly, we did go for it. Well, except for Jackson, but you know what he's like about staying in control. The rest of us were quite merry, as I recall, and you and I had a lovely long chat, sitting in a corner away from the others and then — well — '

'We kissed?' Izzy's face felt as if it were on fire. 'Seriously? Golly, I'm mortified.'

'Oh, charming.' Ash turned away from her and put his glass on the coffee table. 'You certainly know how to flatter a chap.'

Izzy giggled nervously. 'Sorry, Ash. I didn't mean it like that. Just — oh!' Now that she came to think about it, there was a sudden stirring in the recesses of her memory. Only vague recollections, nothing solid, but there just the same. He wasn't making it up, that was for certain. 'How come you never mentioned this before?'

Ash shrugged. 'You never said anything about it afterwards, and I guessed that you wanted to forget. I hadn't realised you really had forgotten.' He rolled his eyes. 'There was I, hoping it would be the start of a beautiful friendship, pining away when you didn't say anything when we went back to work, and all the time you'd forgotten I even existed.'

'I didn't forget you existed!' She reached for his hand. 'You've always been on my radar, Ash. Always.'

Why had she even said that? She hadn't lusted after Ash all this time, after all. It wasn't as if he'd been the object of her affections for years, or that she'd gazed longingly at him across the hall during school assembly, wishing he'd notice her. Nothing like that. Ash had just been — well — *there*. A good, gifted teacher. A kind man. A fun colleague. Someone to trust, talk to, rely on . . .

She blinked as he turned back to her, suddenly noticing that he was actually a very attractive man. How had she not realised that before? How could she ever have forgotten that he'd kissed her? She couldn't imagine that, if he kissed her again, she would ever forget it.

Maybe there was only one way to test that theory.

Izzy wasn't sure, afterwards, if she'd subconsciously communicated her desires to Ash and he'd moved towards her in response, or if she'd unthinkingly moved towards him. Maybe it was mutual. Whatever had happened, somehow his arms were around her and they were sharing a kiss that Izzy just knew would be imprinted on her memory forever.

'Well,' she breathed, when he finally released her, 'I'm not likely to forget that in a hurry!'

'I'm very glad to hear it,' he murmured. 'Though, I have to tell you, there's a lot more where that came from.'

Izzy thought that was very good news indeed. It was, after all, always best to be sure about these things.

7

The weekend couldn't come soon enough for Ash. It had been an excruciatingly long two days since he and Izzy had kissed, and her attitude at school the following morning had only proved that his darkest fears had been confirmed. She obviously bitterly regretted that she'd gone along with it and wanted only to forget that it had ever happened — much as she'd forgotten that long-ago kiss. Just like the last time, she was acting as if it had never happened — except this time she couldn't possibly say she was too drunk to remember it.

Ash tried to tell himself it was for the best. Izzy was still recovering from her break-up with Matt, and the last thing he needed or wanted was to be a rebound fling. Besides, it was never a good idea to have a relationship with a colleague. He knew that only too well. After his broken seven-hour engagement, it had become quite clear that he couldn't be around his ex-fiancée and, since she was a teacher at the same school, he'd felt obliged to look for another job, which was how he came to be working at Bramblewick in the first place. He certainly didn't want to have to leave the little primary school that he'd grown to love, along with a job that made him extremely happy.

If he and Izzy had got involved things would've bound to become complicated and then where would that have left him? On the hunt for a new job again, because Izzy lived in this village. Her friends were here. She'd grown up here. It would be him who had to look elsewhere, not her.

Even so, it was painful to endure her obvious attempts to keep him at a distance. Rehearsals had been awkward and uncomfortable, with Izzy standing at one end of the hall dealing with one group of pupils, while he was over at the other side with the other group. It was as if she'd constructed an invisible wall between them, determined to keep him at arm's length. Ash couldn't deny that it hurt.

He was too embarrassed to even tell Jackson what had happened. Friday night had come as a blessed relief, and he drove home determined to spend the entire weekend without a single thought of Izzy in his head.

On Saturday, Ash couldn't dispel the gloom that descended on him from the moment he opened his eyes. Unable to settle to anything, he decided to brave the crowds at Helmston Market and buy the Christmas decorations for his flat. At least he could cheer the room up, even if he couldn't manage it with himself.

Stepping outside the flat, he fumbled with the key, his fingers already numbing with the cold. He glanced up at the sky which was dark and threatening. It matched the ice that was forming in his heart, he thought, then laughed to himself at his dramatic musings. *Get a grip, Ash. It was one kiss!* Except, it hadn't been. It had been several kisses, each one more passionate and more wonderful than the last. If Izzy hadn't had to get back to Bramblewick, if it hadn't been a work day the following morning, who knows what might have happened?

Good job it hadn't, he thought wretchedly. If a few kisses had made her this jumpy, he could only imagine how she'd have reacted if they'd done anything else.

The market place was heaving, as he'd expected. The bitter cold did nothing to deter the eager Christmas shoppers on the hunt for a bargain. Ash didn't want to linger longer than he had to. He knew where he was heading and, once his business was concluded, he was going straight home. He was glad that he only lived a couple of streets away from the market. It made shopping such a quick and relatively painless process.

The stall that he'd visited a couple of

weeks ago, when he'd purchased the Christmas cards for his pupils was, as he'd feared, surrounded by eager customers. Ash had to push his way through the excited throngs to peruse the collection of baubles, tinsels garlands and lights that sat enticingly on the stall. He wasn't worried about the safety of the products. He knew most of the traders in the market, and the man who owned this stall was a regular, selling occasion cards and gifts throughout the year. He'd been a stallholder at the market for years with no trouble.

He didn't need any lights, nor many baubles for his tree, although he liked to get a couple of new ones every year. It was mainly decorations for the flat that he'd decided to buy. The rooms were big and needed some Christmas cheer to fill them up. He soon had a couple of carrier bags full of garlands and other items that would, at any other time of year, be labelled tat and thrown into the dustbin.

He'd even managed to get hold of a

Nativity scene which would look nice on the fireplace, he thought. He remembered Izzy's tactful words about his electric stove and gave a rueful smile. He'd bet her little cottage was decorated beautifully and tastefully, with none of this cheap rubbish to diminish its charm. Oh, well. He didn't live in an old, traditional cottage, did he? He lived in a large, modern flat, and it was horses for courses.

He thanked the stallholder and turned away, his nostrils twitching at the smell of the nearby food van selling roast pork and turkey sandwiches. He was suddenly reminded of how hungry he was. Even so, he was only a five-minute walk from home. He could get something to eat when he got in. Couldn't he?

Deciding he deserved a treat and realising he was, after all, only human, Ash hurried over to the stall and took his place in the queue, digging around in his pockets for loose change.

'Given in to temptation?'

He jumped, his face beginning to burn as he realised Izzy was standing directly in front of him. She was the last person he'd expected to see, and the shock of her presence made him tongue-tied. 'Er, yeah. Always.'

Not the most tactful of things to say in the circumstances, he realised, wincing inside as she eyed him steadily. At least she wasn't avoiding him today, which was something to be grateful for, he supposed.

'I couldn't resist either,' she told him, her voice loaded with meaning.

Ash was totally confused. What was she up to? Why was she speaking to him today when she'd acted like he was invisible at school? 'Right,' was all he could manage.

She nodded at the carrier bags. 'Been buying Christmas decorations, I see,' she said, obviously noting the foil garland that was sticking out of the top of one.

'Er, yeah, I thought I'd decorate the flat this afternoon. Cheer the place up a bit.' *And cheer me up, too, with any luck.*

'I've been shopping down Castle Street,' she informed him, rattling a carrier bag. 'Just bits and bobs. I've done most of my Christmas shopping and the cottage is already decorated. I got my tree up last night.'

'Great. Well done.' He didn't know what else to say.

Izzy hesitated a moment, then she turned back to the stall. Ash groaned inwardly. He hadn't exactly sounded friendly, but he was flummoxed, truth to tell. He wasn't sure what she wanted, and he was terrified of saying or doing the wrong thing.

Izzy took her roast turkey sandwich from the stallholder and handed over the money. As she turned around, she smiled uncertainly at Ash. 'Right, well, see you on Monday then.'

'Izzy!'

She stopped, eyeing him with what he was almost certain was hope.

'What can I get you?' The stall holder

145

sounded impatient, mindful, no doubt, of the long and very hungry queue that was growing longer with every minute behind Ash.

'Yes?' Izzy said.

'Turkey and stuffing sandwich, is it?' The stallholder demanded.

'Would you — I mean, if you like — '

'Or pork and apple, maybe?' The stallholder tutted. 'Look, mate, make your mind up, will you? Soon be Christmas, you know.'

'Sorry, yeah.' Ash blinked, and Izzy moved away. Feeling stupid, he ordered a turkey and stuffing sandwich and waited, head down, wondering why he'd let Izzy out of his sight for the sake of a stupid sandwich, when he could have walked home in five minutes and made one in his own kitchen.

Furious with himself, he handed over the money and walked away from the stall, the carrier bags in one hand and the sandwich in the other.

'So,' said a voice in his ear, 'would I what?'

Ash found that he was smiling and couldn't seem to help it. Izzy took a large bite out of her sandwich and raised an eyebrow, waiting for his answer.

'Would you like to eat that at my place? I could make us a hot chocolate, too.'

He held his breath and then exhaled slowly as she gave him a wide grin.

'You just want cheap labour, don't you? You want me to decorate your flat for you, all for the price of a hot chocolate.'

'Maybe,' he said, feeling a sudden lightness and warmth at the twinkle in her brown eyes. 'Do we have a deal?'

'I think we do,' she said.

They hurried back to his flat, chatting about the stall and the market and the general quality of Christmas decorations. As they reached the front door, Ash fumbled for his keys and Izzy took the carrier bags and sandwich from him, allowing him to open the door more easily.

'Izz?' The door was half open, but he had to ask, before he let her in — before he made a total fool of himself or scared her away for good.

She was shivering, and he was glad he'd got the central heating on. 'Yes?'

'The other night — it was great.'

She looked worried. 'I thought so. What do you want to tell me? That it was a big mistake?'

'No!' *God, anything but.* And yet . . . 'I don't get it. You gave me the cold shoulder at work the next day and I just don't know what you want.'

She sighed, gazing down at her half-eaten sandwich for a moment. 'Thing is,' she admitted eventually, 'I was worried. I thought, maybe this is a really bad idea. Working together, getting involved. It could go horribly wrong.'

'It could,' he agreed softly. 'So, what's today all about?'

She shrugged. 'Maybe,' she said eventually, 'despite all the problems it may incur, I just can't resist you.' She looked up to the dark sky and pulled a face as the first drops of rain began to fall.

Ash pushed open the door. 'Let's go inside and get warmed up,' he said. 'I'll make you that hot chocolate and we can start to transform this flat into something a bit more festive.'

'Ash,' she said, her eyes seeming suddenly very large in her pretty, heart-shaped face, 'is this okay? Is it what you want?'

He tilted her chin, lifting her face to his, and answered her question with a kiss. Words, he decided, were sometimes very overrated.

8

'Quiet, everyone! Quiet!'

Ash clapped his hands and the children turned towards him. Izzy looked around, smiling to herself at the obvious buzz of excitement in the hall. It was their first full rehearsal and expectations were high — at least in some quarters. She could only cross her fingers and hope that it didn't turn out to be a total disaster, although Ash seemed fairly confident.

'They've all been really good about learning their lines, and they're enjoying themselves. It will be okay,' he'd told her, the previous evening, as they'd sat together on the sofa at Rose Cottage. They were supposed to be watching a film, but Izzy was far too nervous to concentrate. There weren't many rehearsal days left and if it all went pear-shaped . . .

'It won't,' Ash promised her. 'Stop worrying.'

She'd nodded and snuggled against him, feeling a sudden contentment. Outside, darkness had fallen, and the air was freezing cold. In the living room of Rose Cottage, though, the flames danced merrily within the wood burner, the lamplight cast a cosy glow around the room, and all was snug and warm. The Christmas tree lights twinkled, and holly and mistletoe added to the festive feel, with one very convenient sprig of mistletoe pinned above the front door, so that every time Ash entered the cottage he was compelled to kiss Izzy or suffer the consequences.

'There's something missing in here,' he'd said, looking around him with a puzzled expression the first time he'd visited after their meeting in Helmston. 'What is it?'

'The armchair,' Izzy said. 'It was either that or the Christmas tree and the Christmas tree won. One of the drawbacks of a small cottage, I'm afraid.'

'So, where's the chair?'

'Upstairs in the spare bedroom, sitting on top of the bed.'

'You should have asked me to help you take it up there!'

'It's okay. Rachel came round and we managed it together.' Seeing his blank expression, she smiled. 'Rachel's my friend. She works at the surgery with Anna, although she's a nurse, not a receptionist. She's engaged to Xander North.'

'Ah, I know who you mean.' Ash nodded. 'She's Sam Johnson's mum, right? How's Anna doing, by the way? That baby can't be far off arriving now, although you'd never know it from Gracie.'

'She's due a few days before Christmas.' Izzy shrugged. 'I'm sure she's fine. I haven't really had time to visit her, I've been so busy.'

And Anna hadn't called her either, she realised gloomily. There'd been little communication between them since that meal at Chestnut House.

How had things gone so badly wrong? As if she didn't know.

'You should go and see her,' Ash said. 'It's an important time for her. I'm sure she's missing her best friend.'

Not as much as you might suppose, Izzy thought. She smiled. 'Yes, I must. Anyway, about this rehearsal . . . '

Izzy blinked, back in the room as Jackson strode past her, looking quite determined. In his hand he carried the sheet music for the Christmas carols. 'Let's do this thing,' he said, sounding grim as he headed to the piano.

Izzy and Ash exchanged glances and he winked at her reassuringly. Izzy took a deep breath and addressed the children. 'Okay, guys, this is it. Our first full rehearsal. If this goes well then, on Wednesday, we'll do a full dress rehearsal. Now, you all know your lines and you know the songs, so this should be a doddle for you all.'

She smiled at them as they exchanged nervous glances. 'Above all, let's have some fun, eh?'

They all nodded and there were some nervous giggles and a few nudges, as Ash called for them to get into their positions.

A very solemn Liza Meadows stepped onto the stage. She was the narrator and duly set the scene as, behind her, Benjy strode up and down the stage, his expression clearly demonstrating that Scrooge was not a man to be messed with. As two of the Year Four pupils rattled their charity collection boxes at him, he roared, 'Humbug!' at the top of his voice and gave them a scowl that was Oscar-worthy. Izzy grinned, suddenly feeling more relaxed.

Jackson began to play the introduction to 'Once in Royal David's City' and a group of children from Years Five and Six stepped forward to sing. Izzy felt rather emotional, although the carol obviously didn't have the same effect on Ebenezer Scrooge, who rewarded the choir with a roar of disapproval when they'd finished, and left them clearly startled as he marched off towards the orphanage, which he owned.

The stage became more crowded as Sara and Josh, who were playing housekeeper Mrs Cratchitt and orphanage manager, Fagin, begged Scrooge for extra rations for the starving orphans, who were all gathered around nodding and trying to look pleading. Some of the little ones were giggling, and Izzy put her finger to her lips to warn them to focus.

Jackson, who was in charge of the musical soundtrack, managed to get the first tune, 'Have a Heart, Mr Scrooge', to play just in time and Izzy tapped her foot and nodded encouragingly as Mrs Cratchitt, Fagin and the orphans burst into song.

'I'll go and get Gracie from her classroom,' Ash whispered a few minutes later, and she gave him a thumbs up, her attention focused on the stage as the ghost of Scrooge's ex-business partner, Bill Sykes, rattled his chains and issued dire warnings to Ebenezer.

Jackson, who was in complete charge of the accompanying soundtrack, pressed play on the CD player. Young Freddie Smith, who was playing Bill, began to sing his heartfelt plea to Scrooge to mend his ways, 'Before it's Too Late', in a voice that was sadly rather flat on occasion — a fact that Izzy and Ash had decided could be overlooked, due to his enthusiasm and acting talent.

Gracie showed no trace of nerves as she and Ash entered the hall. She took her place at the side of the stage and, although Izzy couldn't see her from where she was standing, she knew that the young girl would be waiting patiently, her entire focus on her cue. Ash would be with her, just in case, but Gracie loved performing so much that Izzy had no doubts that she would shine. Sure enough, Gracie's entrance was bang on cue and she clearly relished her role as Nancy, the Ghost of Christmas Past.

As she proceeded to take Ebenezer back to his unhappy childhood, Izzy thought how proud Anna and Connor were going to be. She really hoped that

Anna's baby wouldn't arrive before the play happened. She'd hate for Anna to miss this, she thought. She decided that, come what may, she would visit Chestnut House within the next couple of days and check up on her friend. They'd been close for so many years that she couldn't let their friendship evaporate. It had to be worth saving, didn't it?

She straightened, bringing her attention back to the stage, where Nancy was reminding Scrooge of how badly he and Bill Sykes had treated a young woman who had arrived at the orphanage with a tiny baby in her arms, begging for their help. They had sent her away and kept the baby, Oliver Twist, so that, like all their other children, he could be put to work in their factory as soon as he was old enough. The young mother wept and pleaded with them not to take her child away, but they refused to listen, and the poor girl died in the street as Gracie sang 'A Cruel Heart' in a voice so sweet and pure that even the little ones stopped whispering to each other and looked up, listening intently. No doubt about it, Gracie was going to be the star of the show.

At Bill Sykes's funeral, attended by only the gravediggers, the vicar, and Scrooge, Gracie beckoned Ebenezer past a group of Year Four carol singers outside the 'church', and led them in the carol, 'God Rest Ye Merry Gentlemen'. Izzy blinked away the tears. Anna was going to sob her heart out to this.

Gracie's part complete, Ash took her back to her classroom as Theo West, a cheerful nine-year-old with a face full of freckles, took centre stage as Bob Cratchitt — the Ghost of Christmas Present.

He was well-cast, Izzy thought, a wide grin on her face as Theo *ho ho ho*-d and thigh-slapped and back-clapped and generally had a jolly good time, while showing Scrooge how other people celebrated Christmas.

Ebenezer's nephew and his wife were

having a fine feast and raised a glass to toast their miserable uncle. Across London, a lonely and heartbroken old man sat at a fine table, as his sad housekeeper served dinner. On the wall behind them hung a portrait (or rather, a photograph, but Izzy hoped the audience would overlook that) of little Oliver Twist's mother, causing Scrooge to feel unfamiliar pangs of conscience.

Back at the orphanage, Fagin sent Dodger and some of the other orphans out to steal as much food as they could from the wealthy, and Mrs Cratchitt turned a blind eye to their wrongdoings, glad to be able to serve a relative banquet to her charges for once. She and Fagin led the orphans in a rousing rendition of a cheerful song called 'A Christmas Feast'.

Little Oliver, however, was too poorly to eat much, and as the song faded away, Mrs Cratchitt hurried over to him, telling Fagin she feared for his life. As the Ghost of Christmas Present confirmed to Scrooge that he could see an empty bed where Oliver now lay, Mrs Cratchitt got all the little orphans into bed, and they broke into 'Away in a Manger'. One by one, they drifted off to sleep, until only Mrs Cratchitt herself was left to sing the line *bless all the dear children in thy tender care.*

Never mind Anna, thought Izzy, she was going to be a blubbering mess herself at this rate. She looked up as Ash came to stand by her side.

'Are you okay?'

Izzy nodded. 'Yes, it's just — well, it's more emotional than I expected.'

He smiled, seeming to understand. 'They're doing so well, aren't they?' he whispered, nodding at the little Foundation Year pupils who were curled up on the floor, their begged for and borrowed bedding pulled over their little forms. As they'd been instructed, they kept perfectly still, feigning sleep as Mrs Cratchitt and Fagin finished the carol, while Ebenezer wiped away tears as he stood watching with Bob Cratchitt's ghost.

'This is brilliant,' Izzy said, feeling a lump in her throat. 'I'm so proud of them.'

'Imagine what it's going to be like when they're in full costume,' Ash said, his voice loaded with excitement. 'The parents are going to love it.'

As the pupils filed off stage, one little form didn't move. Izzy and Ash glanced at each other, then hurried towards the worryingly-still child. Izzy's heart was in her mouth as Ash jumped onto the stage and pulled back the blanket to reveal the tousled blonde head of a little girl, who Izzy recognised as four-year-old Kara Edlinton.

Ash smiled at Izzy and shook his head, then he gently picked up the sleeping child. 'Come on, sweetheart,' he murmured, 'time to wake up. You were a bit *too* convincing there.'

9

Anna's face lit up when she saw Izzy standing at the door.

'I wondered where you'd got to! I'm so pleased to see you. Come in, come in. It's freezing out there.'

She stepped back and ushered Izzy into the hallway, although it was a tight squeeze to get past her huge bump. Izzy almost commented that it seemed to have grown even larger since she'd last seen her, but, remembering Anna's sensitivity levels, decided not to mention it. She was just relieved that Anna seemed glad to see her as she'd been half convinced that the door would be slammed in her face.

'Gracie's in the living room with Connor, watching a DVD, so shall we go into the kitchen?'

Izzy frowned. 'Will you be comfy there?'

'Oh absolutely. I can just about squeeze onto the wicker chair by the French doors. That's if you don't mind sitting on one of the other chairs? I know they're a bit hard on the posterior.'

'I don't mind,' Izzy said. 'Shall I put the kettle on?'

She held her breath for a moment, hoping that Anna wouldn't demand to know why she thought her incapable of doing it for herself, but to her relief Anna sighed and sank down into the wicker chair saying, 'That would be great, Izz. Thanks.'

The kitchen door opened, and Connor popped his head around. 'Hello, Izzy. Great to see you.' He cast an anxious look at Anna. 'Are you all right in here? Are you comfortable enough?'

Anna smiled. 'I'm fine, and if I get uncomfortable I'll come through to the living room, don't worry.'

He hesitated, then nodded. 'Okay, well if you need anything — '

'I'll be sure to yell,' his wife confirmed, rolling her eyes.

Izzy gave him a sympathetic look. He was only looking out for her, after all. 'I'm just making a drink, Connor,' she told him. 'Do you want one?'

He shook his head. 'Just had one, thanks. I'm going to let Gracie finish this DVD then she can go to bed and I'll get on with some paperwork. She's yawning already, but she won't give in until she's seen the whole film, even though she's seen it at least a dozen times already.'

'She's had a tiring few days,' Izzy said, dropping teabags into mugs. 'Rehearsals are exhausting.'

Connor nodded. 'How's she doing?' he asked.

'Absolutely brilliantly,' Izzy assured him. 'Now that we've made sure she only gets called from the classroom just before it's her turn to go on, she's doing really well.'

'Thanks for that, Izz,' Anna said.

Izzy shook her head. 'Ash's idea,' she

told them. 'He's so good with her. He's good with them all. He's amazing.'

She realised that Anna and Connor were exchanging knowing glances and blushed. Connor grinned. 'I'll leave you to it then,' he said and closed the door behind him.

Anna could hardly wait to pounce. 'Go on then!' she said immediately. 'What was that all about?'

'What was all what about?' Izzy feigned innocence and collected the milk from the fridge.

'Don't give me that!' Anna tilted her head to one side and put on a simpering expression. 'Ash is so good with absolutely everybody. He's just amazing!'

'Give over! I didn't say that,' Izzy protested. 'And I certainly didn't use that silly voice.' She carried the mugs of tea over to where Anna was sitting, placing one on the occasional table beside the wicker chair, and the other on the table. Pulling out a chair she sat and faced her friend, trying to look nonchalant, though knowing from experience that it wouldn't work.

'I want to know everything,' Anna said.

'About what? The play? Well, it's a mashup of — '

'Not the play!' Anna tutted. 'You won't get away with it, you know, so you may as well tell me now.'

Anna had always been able to read her like a book, Izzy mused, knowing the game was up. 'Okay, well, if you must know, I've been seeing Ash.'

'I knew it!' Anna clapped her hands together in excitement. 'Didn't I tell you, right from the off? Oh, I'm so glad, Izzy. He's such a lovely bloke. But when did it happen? How?'

Between sips of tea, Izzy relayed the story of how she and Ash had become involved. Anna listened intently, nodding now and then and breaking in with the odd, *ah*, or *how lovely*.

'Fancy you forgetting that he'd kissed you,' she said eventually. 'You must have been very drunk.'

'I must've been,' Izzy admitted,

shamefaced. 'Probably the relief at having survived the residential trip in one piece.'

'Poor Ash,' Anna mused. 'To think, he was waiting all that time for you to mention the kiss, and you'd forgotten all about it.'

'I know.' Izzy pulled a face. 'Still, it's all in the past now.'

'And you're looking to the future?' There was a question mark in the sentence and Izzy hesitated, not sure how much she wanted to say or if, indeed, she knew for certain what it was she wanted.

'We're just taking it one day at a time,' she said eventually. 'Enough of all this, anyway. How are you? That's what I really came to find out.'

Anna sighed, shifting position in the chair. 'I'm all right, just bored. These last few weeks have really dragged and I'm missing work. Connor says he and Riley have whittled the GP candidates down to three and they're coming back for a second interview and a look around this week. I'm dying to have a look at them.' She tutted. 'I'm even missing all the filing, can you believe, and that's my least favourite job in the world. Shows how fed up I am.'

'That will soon pass when the baby arrives,' Izzy reassured her. 'It's all this hanging around, waiting, that's getting you down. When the little one arrives, you'll be so busy you'll forget all about work.'

'I suppose so.' Anna gently patted her bump. 'I wish my mum and dad were around to see this little chap when he finally makes an appearance. They would have loved him. Or her.'

'I know,' Izzy said softly. Anna had lost her mother when she was just a little girl, and her father, who had been the village doctor, had died unexpectedly just a few years ago. Since then, Anna had met Connor, fallen in love, got married and was now expecting her first child. It must be a huge source of grief to her that neither of her parents were around to see how happy she was.

She thought about her own parents, enjoying themselves to the full in the south of Spain. She was glad they were still around and glad that they were happy. Life could be very unfair at times. She'd received a text from her mum only that morning, asking her if she wanted to fly out to join them for Christmas. She hadn't replied yet. She would have to speak to Ash about that. She realised suddenly that she had no idea about his parents, or his plans for Christmas.

'Anyway, Connor suggested that, if it's a boy we name him Arthur, after my dad, and if it's a girl, Eloise after Mum.'

'That's a lovely idea,' Izzy said. 'Your parents would be thrilled.'

'I know.' Anna sipped her tea, deep in thought, then she shook her head slightly and smiled. 'Anyway, enough of all this. How's it going with the play?'

Izzy beamed at her. 'It's going wonderfully. We had a full dress rehearsal this morning and, fingers crossed, all went well — at least, mostly.'

'Gracie's the Ghost of Christmas Present *and* Nancy?' Anna wrinkled her nose, looking a little confused.

Izzy laughed. 'It's not two separate roles. In this play, Nancy *is* the ghost. It's a real mashup of *Oliver Twist and A Christmas Carol*. Sounds a bit odd, but it works.'

'I'm sure it does,' Anna said. 'Gracie loves her costume, anyway and I think Connor and I know every word of 'A Cruel Heart'. Is Sam in this play?'

'Oh yes. He's Oliver Twist's grand-father. He's enjoying himself almost as much as Gracie. I think Rachel will be very proud of him, and Xander will be delighted that his future stepson is loving acting so much.'

'I can't wait to see it,' Anna said. She rubbed her back thoughtfully. 'I really hope I don't miss it. This little one had better hang on a few days or, even better, come a bit early.' She stared glumly at the bump. 'If I get much bigger you're going to have to reserve me two seats in the hall.'

Izzy laughed. 'It's not that bad. Well, not quite.'

As Anna stuck her tongue out at her, Izzy felt a bubbling surge of joy. Maybe she'd read Anna all wrong, after all. Maybe — just maybe — things were back to normal between them at last.

★　★　★

'You don't go overboard with the Christmas decorations, do you?' Ash turned to Jackson with a broad grin on his face.

Jackson tutted. 'Too right, I don't. I can't bear all that gaudy tat, can you?'

Ash wondered how he could put it. 'Maybe you ought to see my flat before I answer that.'

'Oh, lord.' Jackson took Ash's coat and hung it on one of the hooks in the hall. Ash glanced down at the shoe rack underneath, noting with amusement the various pairs of shoes neatly polished and lined up like soldiers awaiting inspection.

He turned back to the living room, biting his lip to stop himself from laughing at the tiny Christmas tree that sat on Jackson's immaculately polished sideboard. It was one of those trees that came out of a box ready decorated. When you plugged it in, lights immediately twinkled but there was little else to capture the interest of any spectator. Ash thought about his own haphazardly decorated tree, and Izzy's real tree, with its traditional and eclectic collection of baubles, and rather pitied Jackson.

'Cup of coffee?' Jackson queried, heading through to the kitchen which, Ash knew from previous visits, would be gleaming, with not so much as a spoon out of place.

'Cheers. Why not?' Ash glanced out of the window at the sleet grey sky. 'It's forecast snow, you know,' he called through the open door. 'They say it's going to be a bad winter. It certainly feels cold enough today.'

'Have you really come round to talk about the weather?' Jackson came back into the living room, his eyebrows raised.

'Of course not. I was just making an observation, that's all.'

'Hmm.' Jackson sank into the black leather sofa. 'Kettle's boiling. So, Ash, to what do I owe this unexpected pleasure?'

'We only live three streets away from each other, mate,' Ash pointed out. 'It's not like I felt I needed to book.'

'Even so.' Jackson eyed him curiously. 'We usually pre-arrange these things.'

'That's because you're a control freak,' Ash said, amused. 'You like to pencil every last thing into that diary of yours. Bet it really freaked you out when that doorbell rang.'

Jackson ran a hand through his hair. 'Okay, you're being sarky and rude for no good reason, and you've turned up on my doorstep without warning and seem to have nothing of any importance to tell me. Let me guess, there's a woman involved.'

Ash gaped at him. 'Certainly not! I

mean, I haven't — I mean — '

'So that's a yes, then.' Hearing the click of the kettle, Jackson sprang to his feet. 'Hold that thought,' he told a flustered Ash. 'Be back in a moment.'

Ash sank into the chair and tapped the arm nervously. He hadn't come to discuss Izzy with Jackson. He hadn't come to discuss anything with him, really. He'd just been at a loose end and felt restless and wanted some company. He could have called Izzy, asked if she wanted him to visit, but he didn't want her to feel crowded. They'd seen each other at least four times that week outside of school and, given that they were spending hours together at rehearsals, he was worried she'd get sick of the sight of him.

Jackson finally returned carrying two mugs of coffee. He asked Ash to hold them while he took two coasters from the sideboard drawer and laid them out on the coffee table, placing the mugs carefully on top of them. Evidently satisfied that no lasting damage would be done to his furniture, he sat down on the sofa and surveyed Ash with an amused expression. 'So, I presume you're here to talk about Izzy?'

Ash's face was on fire. 'How could you possibly . . . ?'

'Oh, please.' Jackson rolled his eyes. 'You think I haven't noticed? You think most of the staff haven't noticed? It's the talk of the staff room.'

'But — we've been so careful.'

Jackson burst out laughing. 'You must be joking! The way you two gaze longingly at each other across a crowded hall it's a wonder you don't just take out a full-page ad in the *Whitby Gazette*.'

'Oh no.' Ash wondered how Izzy would react to this revelation. She'd probably wanted to keep their relationship under the radar as much as he had.

'What's the problem?' Jackson queried. 'Does it matter who knows? You two are an item, and that's great news. Everyone's really pleased for you both. You make a great couple.'

'Do we?' Ash realised he sounded doubtful and cleared his throat. 'I mean, yes, we do. Thanks.'

Jackson leaned forward, his brows knitted together. 'Come on, Ash, what are you worrying about? Things are going okay with her, aren't they?'

Ash took a deep breath. Truthfully, he wasn't sure how good Jackson would be at relationship advice, but he had no one else that he could trust. 'Things are going really well. For now.'

'Right. So, you're dating a girl you've fancied for years — don't try to deny it,' Jackson said, holding up his hand as Ash started to protest. 'Ever since that night in The Monk's Haven your whole attitude towards her has been different. You fell for her that night, mate. I could tell the minute you both got back to the hostel. Whose bright idea was it for us all to go out to Whitby the following night, eh? And who made sure they spent the entire night cosied up with Izzy? And who, of all of us, was the one who kissed her that night, eh?'

Ash cleared his throat. 'Yes, well,' he mumbled awkwardly, 'it may be true that I did have feelings for her at the time.'

'No doubt about it,' Jackson said. 'And I honestly think you've never resolved those feelings. Why else would you be single for so long, if not for the fact that you've been carrying a torch for her all this time?'

'Er, may I remind you that you've been single for just as long as I have?'

'True,' Jackson acknowledged. 'But I haven't met a woman I've wanted to date for a long time. You, on the other hand, clearly have. Come on, just admit it. It's always been Izzy, hasn't it?'

Ash hesitated then shrugged. 'Okay, I hold my hands up. I suppose it has, yes.'

Jackson grinned. 'Excellent. So, now you've got what you wanted, what are you moaning about?'

'I'm not moaning! The thing is — ' Ash tried to think of a way to explain, 'I'm worried that I'm not what, or who, she really wants.'

'Meaning?'

'Matt Jones.' Ash rubbed his face worriedly. 'She was with him for around eight or nine months and they'd even agreed to move in together.'

'So?' Jackson shrugged. 'They didn't move in together, though, did they? It's over, so what's your problem?'

'Have you ever seen Matt Jones?'

Jackson thought about it. 'Not sure. Might have been behind the bar at The Bay Horse one evening when I popped in. Tall, fair haired?'

'That's the one,' Ash said gloomily. 'Looks like a handsome rugby player rather than an average primary school teacher.'

'Oh, please!'

'It's all right for you,' Ash scowled. 'You're not Mr Average, are you? You're a good-looking bloke, too. Not like me.'

Jackson gaped at him. 'Are you serious? Hello!' He waved a hand at his face and said, 'No one ever called me good looking. Have you any idea what I went through when I was a kid?'

Ash had forgotten. The scar on Jackson's lip was faint and, besides, he'd grown a beard which mostly covered any signs that he'd ever had a cleft lip at birth. He realised, for the first time, that the scar was probably the reason for the facial hair in the first place. He'd never given it much thought before. 'But that was years ago,' he said, feeling guilty. 'Truth is, you're a handsome bloke. Whereas I'm . . . ' His voice trailed off as he thought about what he was. Five ten, average build, not muscular, no fan of the gym, hazel eyes, mid-brown hair.

* * *

Nothing distinguished about him at all, he thought. Whereas Izzy — Izzy was stunning. A five-foot four bundle of fun, with warm brown eyes, that sexy blonde bob, and a smile that was brighter and more welcoming than any amount of Christmas tree lights. What could he possibly have done to deserve her?

'Whereas you're, what? Not Matt

179

Jones. She doesn't want Matt Jones, does she? She wants you, or she wouldn't be with you.'

'But does she? What I mean is, why did she and Matt break up? What if it wasn't her decision? What if she hasn't got over him? They were together for the best part of a year. They were going to live together until something went wrong. How do I know she's not on the rebound? That she's not still pining for him. I don't want to be her rebound romance. We all know what happens to those.'

'Do we?'

'Of course we do. Rebound bloke is the one who picks up the pieces when a woman's had her heart broken, helps her heal, then gets dumped when she moves on to the love of her life.'

'Right.' Jackson steepled his fingers under his chin and surveyed Ash with great solemnity. 'You're quite right. It's a catastrophe waiting to happen. You're doomed.'

Ash was appalled. 'Oh, great! Thanks.'

'Well, sorry, but now that you've said it I don't know why I didn't think of it before. This Matt Jones was obviously a big part of Izzy's life, and she needs someone to help her through it. Once she's recovered she's bound to move on and leave you behind. Stands to reason.'

Ash felt sick. 'But, surely, there's a chance that I might be the one she needed all along?'

Jackson looked highly doubtful. 'Doesn't work like that, does it?'

'Sometimes it does,' Ash protested. 'Matt may have been completely the wrong man for her and, after all, Izzy and I have loads in common.'

'Do you?'

'Yes, we do!' Ash was quite stung by the dubious tone in Jackson's voice. 'We both love teaching for a start. Then there's our taste in houses. You should see her cottage, Jackson. It's amazing, honestly. And she loves my furniture. Says it's exactly to her taste. Do you know, we both say bangers and mash is

181

our favourite meal, and we even take our tea the same way. And then, of course, there's — '

Jackson's laughter cut him off from saying any more.

'What's so funny?' he asked indignantly.

Jackson shook his head. 'You really have to ask? Come on, what have you just said?'

Ash was quiet for a moment, then he gave a sheepish laugh. 'I guess I've answered my own questions, haven't I?'

'Yes, I think you have.' Jackson sighed. 'Look, Ash, no one knows what the future will bring, and no relationship comes with guarantees, but you and Izzy have got a good chance of making this work. So what if Matt Jones looked like a blond Adonis?' His eyes crinkled at Ash's expression. 'Okay, maybe not an Adonis, but still. What does it matter? He's out of the picture. Izzy's not with him anymore. She's with you. Now stop being a wuss and go for it. What the heck have you got to lose?'

My pride, my dignity, my heart. Ash sighed inwardly. Whatever the risk, he was in too deep to back out now. Izzy meant far too much to him. He could only hope that Jackson was right.

10

Sam was gasping for breath. He lay, one hand on his chest, making the most disturbing noises as Evie Abbot dabbed her eyes at his bedside. Suddenly, Sam made a dramatic choking sound and slumped, his hand hanging limply at his side.

Evie turned away from him, her handkerchief clutched tightly in her hand as she wailed, 'It was grief! The poor master! Never got over the loss of poor, dear, Elizabeth. He had nothing to live for — nothing! May they finally be reunited and at peace.'

Sam sneezed, and Evie spun round in shock, dropping her handkerchief in the process. 'You ruined that scene,' she told him. 'It's the best I've ever done it, too. Didn't forget a single word, did I, Miss?'

Ash and Izzy grinned at each other as

Sam sat up and protested his innocence. 'I didn't do it on purpose,' he pointed out. 'Them blankets make me sneeze.'

'Well, let's hope they don't make you sneeze on the night,' Izzy said. 'Very well done to you both, though. Excellent deathbed scene there, Sam. Wonderful sound effects.'

Ash put his head down so Sam wouldn't see the amusement in his eyes. The lad had certainly gone to town on his acting, making the most extraordinary noises as he clawed at the air and clutched his throat and rolled his eyes. The script stated that Oliver's grandfather faded away from grief, but Sam certainly hadn't interpreted it that way. Talk about *Do not go gentle into that good night* . . .

At the front of the stage, Benjy yawned, and Abel kicked the floor, looking bored.

'Are we doing Scrooge's funeral now?' he called.

Ash glanced at his watch. 'I think

they've done enough for today,' he murmured to Izzy. 'What do you think? It's your call, after all.'

She gave him a meaningful look. 'Yes, all right, Mr Assistant Director. I think we should probably let them go. They've done really well, and we don't want to overstretch them. Besides, it's only half an hour to the end of school so — ' She raised her head and called to the children. 'That's enough for today, gang. Thanks ever so much for all your hard work. See you on Monday!'

'Only two more rehearsals to go,' Ash said as he and Izzy moved around the hall, collecting discarded costumes and scripts and ushering the children out of the room, reminding them that the bell hadn't yet rung, and they should go back to their classes. 'Feeling confident?'

'Are you?'

He squeezed her hand. 'I'm used to this, remember. This is your first time.'

As a couple of children re-entered the hall he hurriedly dropped her hand.

'Yes, Charlotte?'

The little girl with red hair and freckles put her hands on her hips. 'I'm getting fed up of this lark,' she said abruptly.

Ash looked from her to the other child, Noah, who quickly looked away. 'What lark?' he asked.

'This 'un here,' Charlotte said, gesturing to Noah, 'keeps taking the mick out of me, 'cos I'm playing a lad.'

Ash sighed. 'We've been through all this,' he said. 'There weren't as many traditionally female roles in the play, so we wanted to cast a few of the girls in male roles. Noah, what's your problem with it?'

Noah stuck his chin out defiantly. 'Just think it looks daft. How can a girl be the Artful Dodger? People are gonna laugh at us.'

Ash wondered how a little boy who looked so angelic that he'd been cast as Oliver Twist could sound so aggressive when he chose. 'Is this really what you're concerned about?' he queried.

'Or is that you want Toby to play Dodger?'

Toby was Noah's best friend, and hadn't been given a speaking role, much to his disgust.

Noah tutted. 'Nowt to do with Toby,' he protested, though the colour in his cheeks said otherwise. 'Just think it looks proper daft.'

'Okay.' Ash pretended to consider the matter for a moment, then he clicked his fingers. 'Got it! To balance things up, how about we do this like a traditional panto? So, Charlotte plays Dodger and you, Noah, can play Mrs Cratchitt. I'm sure Sara wouldn't mind being Oliver.'

Noah looked appalled. 'Mrs Cratchitt! No, er, you're all right. Charlotte's okay, I suppose.'

'Really? And you're quite sure you're not going to keep complaining about it?'

Noah nodded frantically, already backing out of the hall. 'No worries, Mr Uttridge. If Charlotte dun't mind, then

I suppose it's all right with me. Just didn't want her to get laughed at, is all.'

'That's very kind of you, Noah,' Izzy assured him.

Charlotte tutted. 'Yeah, and if you believe that you'd believe owt,' she said.

'Problem solved, I think, Charlotte,' Ash told her with a wink.

She grinned at him. 'Ta, Mr Uttridge. See you both on Monday!'

'Well handled,' Izzy said, laughing as the two children shot out of the hall.

'You have to have your wits about you when you're a primary school teacher, don't you?' Ash said, putting his arm around her. 'So, Miss Clark, what are our plans for the weekend?'

Izzy's eyes widened. '*Our* plans?'

Ash felt his stomach churn. 'Sorry. I meant — '

She laughed and nudged him. 'Don't be daft. Why don't we make a whole weekend of it? I'll meet you in Helmston tomorrow and we can do any last-minute present shopping, or go to the pictures, or whatever you fancy. Then come back to Rose Cottage with me and we'll have supper, and — ' she hesitated, 'and then on Sunday we can chill out at my place all day and relax before next week.' When he didn't reply she gabbled, 'I mean, next week is going to be frantic. Last week of term, the play, and the children will already be excited and hyped up for Christmas. I think we're going to need some chill-out time beforehand. If — if you want to, of course.'

Ash tried to keep his voice steady. 'You mean, me stay over on Saturday night?'

Izzy lowered her gaze. 'Only if you want to.'

He lifted her chin and smiled down at her. 'I can't think of anything I want more.'

11

'I suppose I'd better be getting home.' Ash's tone was full of regret. 'I've got some work to do before tomorrow and if I don't go now I'll never leave.'

'Do you have to go?'

Izzy's voice was loaded with disappointment and he crumbled immediately. 'Maybe I could stay for another hour or so,' he conceded.

They snuggled up again, Izzy resting her head on his shoulder as they watched *Miracle on 34th Street* in quiet contentment. In a corner of the room the Christmas tree lights twinkled, and the warmth from the fire seeped through his bones, making him sleepy. This, thought Ash dreamily, was just about the best that life could get. It had been a wonderful weekend, one he would never forget. He hoped it was just the start of many.

His train of thought was broken as

Izzy suddenly turned to him, her eyes shining. 'Just remembered, I forgot to open today's advent calendar door!'

Ash shook his head. 'An advent calendar! Bless you, how old are you?'

'Don't be so grumpy,' she said, jumping off the sofa and rushing over to the living room door where the calendar was pinned. 'Best quality chocolate behind these doors and it gives me a perfect excuse to indulge every single day.'

'Ah, well, in that case . . . ' Ash grinned as she popped the chocolate in her mouth. 'Shouldn't you have offered that to me? I am a guest here, after all, and it's only polite.'

Izzy bounced back onto the sofa beside him. 'You're not a guest here,' she told him.

He kissed her gently. She tasted of chocolate. 'Then what am I?' he murmured eventually.

She stared at him, as if considering her reply, and he waited, his heart thumping.

They both jumped at a loud bang on

the door. Izzy wrinkled her nose. 'Drat. Who on earth's that?'

'Only one way to find out,' Ash said, trying not to feel disappointed that she'd not had the chance to reply to his question. She headed out of the room to the front door and he heard voices. One of them sounded quite panicked. Izzy rushed back into the living room looking flustered.

'What is it?'

'That was Connor. Anna's gone into labour. He wants me to go to Chestnut House to look after Gracie while he takes her to the hospital.'

'Do you want me to come with you?'

Izzy was distracted, unplugging the Christmas tree lights, turning off the television, pulling on her shoes. 'What? Oh, no, of course not. I know you have work to do.'

Suddenly, none of that seemed to matter. 'Gracie might be a bit anxious,' he pointed out. 'You may need some help with her.'

Izzy gave it some thought. 'You're

right,' she said, shrugging on her coat. 'If you're sure you don't mind?'

'Not at all. I'll get my coat.'

★   ★   ★

Hurrying into Chestnut House, some ten minutes later, they found Gracie standing in the kitchen, eyes wide, her hands twisting her hair. Anna, meanwhile, was leaning against the worktop, taking deep breaths. They'd already passed Connor in the hall, carrying Anna's bag to the car.

Izzy rushed over to her friend, rubbing her back sympathetically. Behind her, she heard Ash trying to soothe Gracie. A mixture of cajoling and briskness got her back into the living room, and above the occasional groans from Anna, she could hear him talking to the little girl, obviously trying to distract her.

Connor hurried in, assuring Anna that the engine was running, and her bag was in the boot and was she ready?

Anna looked terrified. 'I don't think

I'll ever be ready for this,' she said, staring at Izzy in terror. 'There's no getting out of it, is there? This baby's got to come out, no matter what.'

'Well, yes, but just think how wonderful it's going to be to hold your child in your arms. In a few hours, Anna, you'll meet your son or daughter. How exciting is that?'

Anna didn't look excited in the least. She looked as if she were bitterly regretting ever trying for a baby.

'Come on, darling.' Connor took her arm, looking panic stricken, despite his medical training. Izzy followed them down the hall, where they paused at the open living room door.

'Won't be long, Gracie,' Connor told his daughter. 'I'll telephone as soon as there's any news, I promise. Be a good girl.' He nodded at Ash. 'Thank you.'

'No problem.' Ash gave Anna a weak smile as she said, 'See you soon, Gracie.'

Gracie stared at her, saying nothing. Izzy saw the couple to the door, wishing Anna the very best of luck and telling them not to worry about Gracie, as everything would be fine here. As the front door closed, she hurried back into the living room, just as Ash said brightly, 'Right, Gracie. What do you want to watch?'

Gracie pursed her lips, thinking for a moment. 'Is Anna going to die?'

Izzy and Ash looked at each other, and Izzy saw her own concern reflected in his face. 'Of course not!' he told Gracie. 'Why would you think that?'

'I've been reading about it. Women do die having babies, you know. Lots of queens and princesses died. I don't want Anna to die.'

Ash sighed. 'The women you've been reading about — that all happened a long, long time ago. Long before there were any hospitals or antibiotics or any of the modern machinery and medicines that we take for granted.'

Gracie looked at him doubtfully. 'So, are you saying that women don't die nowadays?'

Ash hesitated, casting a glance at

Izzy. She gave a slight shrug, not sure what to say. It was true that, even in this day and age, some women did still die in childbirth, but the figures were so low she didn't think it was worth worrying Gracie with. And Gracie would worry, no doubt about it. She would fix on that small number of women and convince herself that Anna would be one of them. Sometimes, honesty wasn't the best policy.

Luckily, Ash seemed to have decided the same. 'Look,' he told Gracie, 'your father is probably one of the best doctors there is. Do you really think he's going to let anything happen to Anna?'

Gracie thought about it. 'Not if he can help it, no.'

'Well, there you are. This is the twenty-first century and we have modern, well-equipped hospitals, full of wonderful doctors like your dad and nurses like Rachel, and no one will be better looked after than Anna. In a few hours, she'll be home again, and you'll have a new baby brother or sister.'

Gracie wrinkled her nose. 'I know.

It's going to cry, isn't it? A lot.'

Ash grinned. 'I'm afraid so.'

Gracie tutted. 'Lucy in my class has got a little brother and she said when he was a baby he cried all the time and she couldn't hear the television. Now he's bigger it's not much better. His toys are all over the floor and she keeps standing on them and hurting her foot.'

'Well, that's kids for you,' Ash told her, laughing. 'When they're babies it's all nappies and teething and crying, and when they're toddlers it's mess and tantrums.' He nudged her. 'It's totally worth it, though. One day, your brother or sister will be a bright, interesting person, just like you.'

Izzy didn't hear Gracie's reply. She rushed into the kitchen, her eyes brimming with tears. *Totally worth it.* That was the way Ash had described having children. She filled the kettle, needing an excuse for her absence from the living room. She could hardly explain to him, if he asked, that she'd been overwhelmed with misery at the realisation that Ash loved kids and was quite obviously looking forward to having some of his own. Why was she surprised? The plain fact was, he was a born father. A natural around children. Look at how he'd dealt with Gracie, not just today but every day at school. Look how he responded to the kids at rehearsals, bringing out the very best in them, spotting the potential in them when other teachers had all but given up. She remembered how he'd defused the situation with Noah and Charlotte the other day, tricking Noah with great humour, no firm tone necessary.

How was he going to react when she told him that she didn't want children? When should she tell him? It wasn't something she could just casually throw into the conversation. She'd been with Matt for nine months before the subject even came up, but she'd been with Ash for a matter of weeks. Maybe it was too soon to even think about discussing it. She didn't even know how serious they were. Yet, she knew, deep down, that there was something special between them, and Ash deserved to know. They both deserved to know where they stood before things went any further. He would have to choose — Izzy or children. She had a sinking feeling that she knew exactly what his decision would be.

'Hey.' Ash wandered up behind her, putting his arms around her waist and resting his chin on her shoulder as she made tea. 'How are you doing?'

She gave a half laugh. 'How am I doing? I'm the least of your worries, surely? Gracie's a mass of anxieties in the living room and poor Anna's in agony at the hospital.' She winced. 'Doesn't bear thinking about.'

'Gracie's watching *Frozen*. We talked, and she's decided she wants a sister, just like Elsa has.'

'Well, in that case, we'd better keep our fingers well and truly crossed for a girl.'

'I suppose we better had,' he agreed. He kissed her on the cheek and took his mug of tea from her hand. 'Anna will be okay, you know.'

'I know.' She shrugged. 'Pretty scary thought, though. Childbirth.'

He nodded. 'I have to say, I'm full of admiration for any mother. Women are definitely the tougher gender.'

Izzy swallowed. 'Anna will be a great mum, though. She's so good with Gracie already.'

Ash sipped his tea. 'And that's no easy task. Hey,' he added, obviously seeing the tension in her face and misreading it, 'cheer up. Anna will be okay, and she'll be bringing that baby home before you know it.'

She gave him a weak smile. 'Yes, I know.'

He put the cup down on the worktop and put his arms around her, pulling her close. As she buried her head in his chest, she heard him murmur, 'Everything will be fine, promise. I love you, Izzy.'

She closed her eyes to hold in the tears. It was the first time he'd ever told her he loved her, and she longed, with all her heart, to say the same words to him but, how could she? Their time together was limited. The minute she told him the truth, it would all be over. The clock was ticking on their relationship, and declarations of love would only make the end more painful for them both.

* ★ ★

'You've got to be kidding me!'

Ash blinked as Izzy's incredulous tone nudged him back into consciousness. He couldn't believe he'd fallen asleep. He rubbed his eyes, noting that Gracie was fast asleep beside him on the sofa. He looked around the room and snapped back to full alertness at the sight of Anna and Connor standing in the doorway, looking very sheepish indeed.

'False alarm,' Anna said. She sounded tired. 'I've never felt so stupid in my life.'

'*You* felt stupid?' Connor sank into

the chair, rubbing his forehead wearily. 'Can you imagine how I felt? All the grins and smirks I got from the staff. *Fancy you not realising it was Braxton Hicks, rather than proper contractions, Dr Blake.*' He shook his head. 'I'll never be able to go back to that hospital, you know. Sorry, Anna, but you're on your own next time.'

'Like heck I am,' she said.

'What's Braxton Hicks?' Ash asked, confused.

'Tightenings of the womb,' Anna said. 'Sort of practice contractions.'

'Sounds grim,' he said.

'They felt real enough to me,' she admitted.

'I'll make you a drink,' Izzy said, getting to her feet.

Anna shook her head. 'Not for me, thanks. I just want to go to bed. I'm shattered.'

'Connor?'

'Me, too,' he admitted. 'I'm so sorry to drag you out for nothing, Izzy. You, too, Ash.'

Ash shrugged. 'No problem.'

'Was Gracie okay?'

Ash glanced at the sleeping child. 'Eventually,' he admitted. 'You might want to have a little chat to her, though, Connor. She's a bit worried about the perils of childbirth. Seems she's been reading up on the subject and she's become quite fixated on the death of Princess Charlotte. You may have to put her mind at rest. I did my best, but — '

'You did brilliantly,' Izzy assured him. 'Probably best that a doctor reassures her, though.'

'Gosh, I never imagined — ' Connor shook his head. 'Poor Gracie. I'll do that tomorrow, after work. Thanks, Ash.'

'We'll get off then,' Izzy said, gathering up hers and Ash's coats. She passed his to him, not looking in his direction. 'I'm glad you're okay, Anna, although sorry it was all for nothing.'

'I should have known really,' Anna said, yawning. 'I was only at the hospital on Friday and they told me there was no sign of the baby being ready to come yet. Nell joked I might have to prise it out with a spoon.'

'Nell?' Izzy's voice sounded sharp. 'Nell went to the hospital with you?'

'Yes. Forty weeks pregnant today, so I had a check-up.' She pulled a face. 'They were talking about what would happen if I went another week. I really hope something happens soon.'

'You should have said. I'd have come with you to the hospital,' Izzy said.

Ash raised an eyebrow. How could she have done that? She was at school that day.

'You work on Fridays,' Anna pointed out.

Izzy folded her arms. 'So does Nell.'

'It's different for Nell. She runs her own business; she can take time off if she wants to. She left Chloe for a couple of hours.'

'How noble of her.'

Ash was bewildered. He'd never heard her sound like that before — almost bitter. Was there something going on that he didn't know about?

If there was, it looked as if Connor didn't have a clue either, judging by the surprised look on his face as he said, 'You all right, Izzy?'

Izzy fastened the belt on her coat and smiled brightly. 'Fine. We'd better get off. You're tired and so are we. We've got a busy day tomorrow with it being the last week of term. And we've got final rehearsals, too. The play's on Wednesday, you know, and there's a lot to do.'

She was gabbling. Ash buttoned his coat, wondering what on earth was going on. Anna, he noted, was saying nothing. She simply sat, watching Izzy grimly. He'd definitely missed something.

Connor showed them to the door, thanking them both again for stepping in to care for Gracie and promising that, next time, he'd make absolutely sure that Anna was genuinely in labour.

They walked in silence to Rose Cottage. The icy air cut through to his bones, but Ash felt that the sudden weird atmosphere between himself and Izzy was far colder. At the cottage door, they stood, depressingly awkward with each other.

'Right, well, I'd better be getting home then,' he said.

Izzy was shivering. 'I suppose you'd better had,' she agreed. 'Sorry you got dragged into babysitting. You'll never get that work done now.'

Ash knew he wouldn't sleep, so had no doubt that he would be able to finish it when he got home. Lord knows what state he'd be in for work tomorrow, though. 'Big week coming up,' he murmured.

She nodded. 'Absolutely.'

'Izzy.' He almost wished he hadn't said her name as she stared at him, her chin buried inside the top of her buttoned-up coat as she struggled to keep warm. 'Back there, at Anna's place — '

'Yes?'

He wanted her to understand, to

reassure him. She said nothing, and he knew he was going to have to bite the bullet. Desperately, he gave a short laugh and kept his tone deliberately light. 'I said I love you, in case it slipped your notice.'

'It's snowing!'

Ash looked up as she cried out, seeing for himself the first gentle flakes of snow drifting down upon them. 'So it is. Way to change the subject.'

Izzy looked at the step beneath her feet. 'Sorry. I know what you said, Ash.'

There was an interminable silence. Ash cleared his throat. 'Right, well, I guess that answers that.'

He turned to head to the car and Izzy's hand shot out, grabbing his arm. 'Ash!'

He looked round, keeping his expression neutral.

'Let's — let's not do this tonight, eh?' she said. 'It's not the right time.'

It was as he'd feared. He was rebound guy — doomed to be passed over when Izzy had fully recovered from her break up with Matt.

'Goodnight, Izz,' he said sadly, not looking back as she closed the front door.

12

Izzy knew that the only person she really wanted to talk to about the mess she had found herself in was her best friend, Anna.

She'd done an excellent job, all day, of avoiding Ash. Because there were only two days left to rehearse the play, they'd decided to focus only on the scenes that were still having teething troubles. They certainly didn't want to overreach the entire cast and felt that the children knew their roles by now and were confident in what they were doing.

The decision had been made, therefore, to simply run through a handful of more tricky scenes, leaving out the songs. It was the last week of term and the children were all very excitable. Classroom activities were pretty hectic, and the arrival of snow had only added to the holiday buzz. Izzy and Ash had decided that they would take it in turns to lead rehearsals, rather than both abandon their classrooms at the same time.

It was, then, quite easy to avoid seeing him for most of the day. She'd gone home for lunch, feeling like a total coward but not knowing what else to do. Ash deserved so much more, and she knew it.

After school, she'd practically sprinted out of the school gates, almost sliding onto her backside as her feet lost their grip in the snow on the pavement outside. She'd rushed home, drawn the curtains, heated up some soup and then settled down to do some serious soap-watching. Unfortunately, her plans for distraction hadn't worked and, after pacing up and down a few times, stuffing her face with several of the chocolate Christmas tree decorations, and flicking mindlessly through the television channels until the remote felt hot in her hand, Izzy gave up and decided to visit Anna.

Anna had called her that morning, before work, and apologised for wasting her time the previous evening. 'I feel such a fool,' she'd confessed. 'I honestly thought that was it. It's scared me to death. If Braxton Hicks are that bad, how painful is it going to be when it's real labour?'

Izzy had winced, glad that Anna couldn't see her face. Her friend had looked pretty uncomfortable last night in the kitchen and goodness only knows how grim childbirth was going to be. Still, no need to let Anna know that. 'I'm sure it's not much worse,' she'd assured her. 'Just different, that's all. And how were you to know it wasn't the real thing? You've never done this before. I'll bet you're not the first mother-to-be who's made that mistake.'

Anna had laughed. 'I suppose not. Connor's feeling even more ridiculous than I am, as well he might. I told him it was all his fault for not spotting the truth! Thanks, Izzy.'

Their relationship seemed to be back

on track, so Izzy wasn't going to spoil it by mentioning how hurt she was that Anna had taken Nell with her to the hospital. Deep down, she knew she was being petty and childish. There was no way she could have taken Friday off work, and of course it was easier for Nell to switch her hours around. Spill the Beans was her own business, after all. She was just being stupid.

Izzy shrugged on her coat, turned off the Christmas tree lights and the television, and headed out into the night to Chestnut House. Snow crunched underfoot as she walked, and before she'd even reached The Bay Horse more fat flakes began to fall. The pub was busy, she realised, hearing the sound of laughter and jolly voices as she passed. It looked quite cosy and inviting through the windows and the fairy lights around the glass did their best to entice her in. She wouldn't mind sitting in there, losing herself in gossip and music and good food and wine. It would be lovely to go for a meal with Ash, she mused, shaking her head slightly at the folly of following that train of thought. *Don't even go there, Izzy*, she told herself, and marched determinedly on towards Chestnut House.

Connor was outside, unloading bags of shopping from the boot of the car.

'She's not been to the supermarket!' Izzy gasped as he stopped rummaging in the boot and grinned at her.

'Don't be daft. As if I'd let her do that. She's inside, Izzy, if you want to go straight in.'

'Do you need a hand?'

'You could take a couple of bags, if you don't mind. I can manage the rest.'

Izzy nodded and carried a couple of bulging carrier bags into Chestnut House, while Connor unloaded the rest of the shopping and slammed the boot shut. She dropped the bags on the worktop in the kitchen, then headed into the living room, only to stop short at the sight before her eyes.

Anna and Nell were curled up together on the sofa, oohing and ah-ing over a bundle of baby clothes. Tiny little babygrows, vests and knitted cardigans were being held up and admired, as if they were designer fashion pieces.

Izzy felt a knot of jealousy in her stomach and fought to stay calm. What on earth was wrong with her? She never used to be like this. But Anna had changed. She was all about babies and children now, and Nell had always been very family-oriented and soppy about things like this.

Izzy and Anna had been close when they were organising Anna's wedding because Izzy loved all that stuff, whereas Nell had no interest whatso-ever in wedding planning. But now, it seemed, things had moved on. Now, it was Nell who had more in common with Anna, and Izzy felt ridiculously left out and hurt. It wouldn't have mattered if Anna hadn't made it very clear that she disapproved of Izzy's decision not to have a child herself, but her friend's judgmental attitude had wounded Izzy, and this felt like the final straw.

Anna and Nell glanced up and saw

her standing in the doorway, and Izzy saw the guilt all over their faces. They immediately began to bundle up the clothes, shoving them back in their plastic bags.

'Nell bought these for the baby,' Anna gabbled. 'Aren't they lovely?'

Nell's face was pink. 'Just a few little things,' she said, smiling far too widely at Izzy. 'Hard to resist buying them, isn't it?'

Since Izzy hadn't bought a single thing for the baby yet, she had to deal with that uncomfortable realisation on top of everything else. She found it hard to sound normal as she replied, 'Obviously, for some.'

Anna managed to haul herself off the sofa. 'I'll put the kettle on,' she said. 'It's good to see you, Izz.'

Was it? Izzy took a deep breath as Nell said, 'Right, well, I think I'll get off home. Riley's cooking supper.' She smiled at Izzy as she passed her. 'Kitchen already smelt fantastic when I left. He's a great cook.'

Well, whoopie-doo, Izzy thought. The perfect man for the perfect Nell. What a perfect life they did live. As she looked into Nell's beaming face, she felt a pang of guilt. Nell was a lovely person, and Riley was a good man. What on earth was wrong with her? 'Enjoy,' she managed.

As Nell bid Anna a farewell, Izzy removed her coat and put it over the back of the armchair before sitting down. She eyed the plastic bags on the sofa mutinously, realising she needed to get herself into gear and buy some presents for the little one who must, surely, be here any day now.

'Don't worry about that,' Anna said, when Izzy voiced her thoughts upon her friend's return. She handed Izzy a mug of tea. 'We've got loads of clothes in newborn sizes, and he won't be in them for five minutes. Best to wait and see if it's a boy or girl before we buy anything else.'

Izzy nodded. 'Right. Will do. Is there anything else you'd like, though?

Anything he needs now?'

Anna shook her head. 'Honestly, we've got far more than we need. Crib, carry cot, travel cot, pram, buggy, car seat, clothes, nappies, bottles, sterilising equipment, toys — '

'Yeah, okay, I get the picture.' Izzy grinned and took a sip of tea.

Anna watched her curiously. 'Are you okay, Izzy? You seem a bit down.'

'Me? I'm fine. I was just at a loose end, so thought I'd come and see how you were doing.'

'After my dramatic, academy-award winning performance of a woman in labour last night?' Anna laughed. 'Feeling stupid, but otherwise fine. Not so much as a twinge today. Think he's taken up permanent residence in here,' she added, patting her stomach.

Connor entered the room, carrying his own mug of tea. 'All done,' he told Anna. 'Everything's packed away. Enough there to feed an army.'

'Have you been buying all your Christmas food?' Izzy enquired.

'Nope. That's just for this week. We've got a delivery booked for the twenty-third. Couldn't face going out to the supermarket so close to the big day. You know how busy it will get, and there's no way Anna's going whether the baby's arrived or not. No, all this food is in honour of my mother's imminent arrival.'

'Dottie's coming to stay?' Izzy smiled. 'How smashing.' Dottie was a lovely woman, kind and generous and very motherly. She'd taken to Anna from the moment she met her and had made no secret of the fact that she hoped she would get together with her son.

'She was going to come for Christmas anyway, but with the baby due she's even more excited. She can't wait.' Anna sighed. 'She's not the only one. I'm really fed up now. This seems to have been going on forever.'

'You've made him too comfortable,' Connor said. 'It's snowing and cold out here. He's probably thinking he's best off where he is.'

Anna rolled her eyes. 'Very funny.'

She turned to Izzy. 'Not with Ash tonight?'

Izzy swallowed. 'Er, no. You know what they say. You can have too much of a good thing.'

'Can you?' Connor sounded doubtful. 'As a doctor, I think I can cheerfully say, when it comes to love you can never have too much.'

'Oh, shut up.' Izzy scrabbled around in her mind for a change of subject. 'Speaking of being a doctor, how are things going at the surgery? Still interviewing for a new GP?'

Connor put down his mug. 'No. We're all sorted. We have a lovely new member of staff and I think the patients are really going to like her. She starts in January, and she's managed to rent a cottage just outside Kearton Bay until she finds somewhere to buy.'

'*She?* We're getting a female doctor? Well, about time.'

'I know! Do you think the residents of Bramblewick are ready for this innovation?' Anna giggled. 'She really is a nice woman, though, Izzy. You'll like her.'

'You've met her?'

'Yes, she came here for an informal introduction, after she'd accepted the post. Met me and Nell and had a nice little chat with us. She's lovely.'

Met her and Nell! But, of course, something else Anna and Nell had in common. Both partnered with the village doctors. Izzy's spirits sank even lower.

'I'm dying to get back to work,' Anna continued. 'It will be great working with a woman doctor, and of course, the surgery looks so different now. Have you seen it since the building work finished, Izzy?'

Izzy couldn't say she had, having been lucky enough to not have a single bout of illness all year.

'It does look amazing,' Connor admitted. 'A much bigger waiting room, new toilet facilities for both the staff and patients, kitchen facilities for the staff, a bigger office and, of course, the new doctor's consulting room.'

'It looks impressive from outside,' Izzy acknowledged. 'How are the patients reacting to the changes?'

Connor gave her a wry grin. 'Well, you know what it's like around here,' he said. 'Some love it, of course, but some are a bit dubious. Don't like change. When I point out that, not that long ago, the surgery was on the point of closure, they soon come around. I'm not sure how some of them are going to react to a female GP, I must admit, but personally, I think it can only be a good thing. Between her and Rachel, our female patients are being well catered for. I know for a fact that some of them have been visiting the Helmston surgery rather than come here because they don't want to discuss certain problems with a male GP. It's frustrating, but understandable, I suppose. This should definitely help those patients out.'

They spent another half an hour discussing the new GP, how much things had changed at the surgery in the last year or so, and reminiscing about Anna's father and how different things had been in Bramblewick back when he was the doctor — at least, Anna and Izzy reminisced while Connor sat and listened quite stoically.

At last, Connor stood up and announced he would have to go to Hatton-le-Dale to collect Gracie from dance class.

'I must be going, too,' Izzy said.

'Really?' Anna looked disappointed. 'Are you sure?'

'I've got a busy day tomorrow,' Izzy told her. 'I need an early night — and I'm pretty sure you do, too.'

'I'll drop you off, Izzy,' Connor said. 'The snow's coming down fast now. It won't take me a minute.'

Izzy nodded gratefully. The truth was, she hadn't intended to leave so early but, sitting here with Anna and Connor, their happiness was only making her realise how much she was about to lose — or had already lost. And how could she talk to Anna about it, when Anna would, no doubt, consider it her own fault? Everyone knew that Ash was a natural with children, and Anna would blame Izzy for the inevitable failure of their relationship. How could she see it any other way? The fact was, there was no way she could tell Anna how wretched she was feeling. She may as well go home and try to get some sleep.

Though, somehow, she doubted very much that sleep would come.

13

Izzy was almost sure she heard Ash calling her name as she headed — as rapidly as she could manage given the slippery surface — out of the school gates towards home.

She'd walked to school that morning, feeling the fresh air would do her good and that the walk would give her a chance to calm down and prepare herself for another day of avoiding Ash. Now, she was regretting that decision. It was snowing again, and the pavements were thick with the stuff, making it less of a walk home and more of a trudge.

She shivered, fastening her coat as high as the zip would allow, and pulling her hood up. Even with gloves on, her fingers felt numb with cold. Winter on the North York Moors could be brutal, she thought, thinking longingly of the wood burner at Rose Cottage. She was glad she'd left the central heating on. The cottage would be warm and toasty.

She didn't often go home for lunch, but the prospect of dodging Ash in the dinner hall was unbearable, so she'd decided to take the coward's way out and leave the school premises.

It took far longer than it usually did to get home, and by the time Izzy left School Lane and stepped into the main street which faced the village green and the beck, she decided that she would definitely have to drive back to work. Blinded by the hood of her coat for a moment, she reached up, pushed it off her face, and stopped dead in her tracks. Ash was outside Rose Cottage. She'd know his car anywhere. Drat!

There was no way she could go home now. Frantically, Izzy tried to think what to do then, hoping Ash wouldn't be looking out of the window for her, she rushed as fast as was humanly possible to Spill the Beans, ducking inside like some hardened criminal on the run from the police.

Being lunch time, the little cafe was heaving, especially as, being so close to Christmas, people were queuing up for baked goods at the counter, too. Nell did a roaring trade in pork pies and Christmas cakes at this time of year, and customers collected them in the run up to the big day, leading to long waits in Spill the Beans.

Chloe, Nell's assistant, was behind the counter looking harassed. Her face was red as she dashed backwards and forwards, trying her best to deal with the increasingly impatient crowd of people who hovered in the shop, muttering about the wait.

'Are you on your own?' Izzy, having finally reached the front of the queue, was puzzled by Nell's apparent absence, especially at such a hectic time.

Chloe blew a wisp of her fringe from out of her eyes and sighed. 'Nell had to take a couple of hours off, so I'm manning the fort like a brave little soldier. What can I get you, Izzy?'

'Er, just a toasted cheese sandwich and a plain latte, please, Chloe. Bit strange that Nell would take time off this week, isn't it?'

Chloe shrugged. 'Couldn't be helped, apparently. Take a seat, Izzy, and I'll be with you as quickly as I can.'

Well, that was a bit abrupt! Was Chloe avoiding the subject? Then Izzy looked around and mentally shook herself. Talk about paranoid! Of course Chloe was being abrupt. There were another five people waiting to be served.

Izzy glanced around, relieved to find one empty table at the far corner of the cafe. She hurried over and dumped her bag on the table, then took off her coat and hooked it over the back of her chair.

One by one, Chloe managed to serve the waiting customers, then she hurriedly fulfilled Izzy's order, bringing the toastie and coffee to her table. She'd barely put the stuff down when the door opened again, and another customer stepped inside. Chloe groaned and rushed back behind the counter, leaving Izzy to tackle her lunch, hoping she'd have time to finish it before she was due back in class.

The little bell above the shop door tinkled again, and Izzy glanced up to see Rachel enter. Glancing round, Rachel caught sight of Izzy and waved before hurrying over. 'What are you doing skulking around in here? Haven't you got a home to go to?' She winked as Izzy chewed on her toastie and shook her head.

'Thought it would make a nice change,' she said, not wanting to go into details about why she really was skulking in Spill the Beans. 'More to the point, what are you doing in here?'

'Thought I'd collect a pasty and take it back to the surgery for lunch. I was late this morning and didn't have time to make anything, and Mum's so loved up with Merlyn she's totally taken her eye off the ball and has quite forgotten she usually makes my pack-up.' She laughed. 'I may have to sack her. Did I tell you, Xander's home tomorrow? So excited.'

'That's great, Rachel. I know you've missed him.'

'I really have. Which reminds me, I'm glad I've caught you, Izzy. Would you mind if I came round to yours tonight to wrap some presents up and leave them in your spare room? Sam's like a sniffer dog when it comes to finding his gifts, and I have a feeling that Xander will be just as bad.'

Izzy couldn't help but smile. She could imagine Xander being a big kid about Christmas. 'No problem. I've got some things to wrap, too, so we can make a night of it.'

'Are you sure? What about Ash?'

Izzy's smile faded. 'What about him?'

'Well, have you got any plans with him tonight? I don't want to spoil anything.'

'No plans for tonight,' Izzy said, managing to sound quite cheerful. 'We're both so full on at work that we've decided to focus on that this week. Present wrapping will be a great distraction.' *Wouldn't it just!*

'That's great. I'll be at yours for around seven. Is that okay?'

'Perfect.'

Rachel beamed at her. 'I'd better go and get that pasty and get back to work. Crikey, it's really busy in here, isn't it?'

'It is,' Izzy confirmed grimly. 'And yet, Nell decides to have today of all days off. Weird or what?'

For a moment, she could have sworn a look of realisation crossed Rachel's face, but then it was gone. 'Must have had her reasons. See you later, Izzy.'

As she hurried towards the counter, Izzy frowned. What was that about? *Golly, Izzy, you really are getting paranoid. You're going to have to get a grip.* She glanced at her watch. And she was going to have to get back to school, too, or she'd be late. She drained her cup, waved her thanks to Chloe, called goodbye to Rachel and shot out into the street. Ash's car was gone, thank goodness. At least she could collect her own car and drive back to school. It would make a clean getaway at the end of the working day easier, too. Whatever else happened, she couldn't risk bumping into Ash and having to deal with *that* conversation. He'd said he loved her, and she hadn't said it back. How on earth was she supposed to explain that?

★　★　★

'Oh, I do love a Christmas carol,' Rachel sighed. 'So soothing and festive. Beats Slade and Cliff Richard any day of the week.'

She and Izzy were sitting on the living room floor at Rose Cottage, surrounded by boxes and bags of all shapes and sizes. Rolls of wrapping paper and packets of gift tags were lying beside them, together with Sellotape and a pair of scissors.

Not to mention, thought Izzy, what looked like the entire contents of Rochester's toy department. How much had Rachel spent on Sam, for goodness sake?

'It's not all for Sam,' Rachel giggled. 'Some of these are for Xander. He does love his gadgets.'

'Good grief.' Izzy shook her head. 'You must be mad.'

'And Sam has had a pretty tough time of it,' Rachel added. 'What with me and his dad splitting up and me moving him all the way up to Bramblewick. He's had to start a new school, make new friends, and get used to Xander. He deserves a smashing Christmas.'

'Sam's doing really well at school,' Izzy assured her, knowing that Rachel had worried to begin with. 'He's made plenty of friends. And he loves Xander, so stop worrying.'

'I'm not worrying. At least, not now.' Rachel gave a sigh of pure contentment. 'I suppose, the thing is, everything's going so well that I keep thinking something will spoil it.' She nudged Izzy. 'I expect you feel the same, what with the way things are with you and Ash. Talk about loved up. I'm so pleased for you.'

Izzy kept her head down as she busied herself with wrapping paper. 'Yes, well, it's early days.'

'But he's such a lovely man,' Rachel continued. 'You two are perfect for each other.'

'Mince pie?' Izzy said brightly. 'I think it's time we had a break, don't you? I'll make us a hot chocolate to go with it.'

She jumped up before Rachel could agree or disagree, and hurried into the kitchen, where she busied herself heating milk on the hob and rummaging in the cake tin for mince pies.

As she carried the hot chocolate and mince pies through to the living room, she stopped for a moment, taking in the festive scene before her. The flames flickered in the wood burning stove, and the Christmas tree lights added a merry glow to the room, while the carols playing in the background only added to the warm, certain knowledge that the big day was almost upon them.

'I do love this time of year.' Rachel stood, rubbed her aching back and took the mug from Izzy's hands with a grateful smile. 'It's going to be our best Christmas yet. This time last year I was living in fear with Grant, and now look at me. I'm so lucky. I couldn't be happier.'

'You deserve it,' Izzy said, meaning it. Rachel had been through a tough time with her ex, Grant, who had made her life a misery. It had taken Rachel many years and a lot of courage to finally make the break from him, and the fact that her bravery had taken her into the path of Xander, one of the kindest-hearted men Izzy knew, seemed like a fitting reward. Together, they had turned the run-down Folly Farm, Rachel's family home, into a happy, busy place again. Xander had a heart of gold and could never say no to an animal in distress, and the farm was once again home to a variety of animals: a horse, two goats, two dogs, a cat, a pony and — just recently — four unwanted guinea pigs, two rabbits and a donkey called Ned. It was the life Xander and Rachel wanted, and they deserved every moment of their new-found happiness.

'Everyone deserves it,' Rachel assured her, then her face fell. 'Well, maybe not everyone,' she amended, probably thinking of Grant. 'Have you met Holly's boyfriend yet, by the way?'

Izzy narrowed her eyes. 'Quick change of subject. No, I haven't. Have you?'

Rachel looked thoughtful. 'Nope. Don't you think that's odd? I'd have thought Holly would have rushed to introduce him to us, since she's so smitten with him. He's certainly spoiling her with evenings out and presents, and she can't gush about him enough at work but — '

'But what? You don't really think he's married, do you?'

Rachel sighed. 'Maybe I'm over-thinking things. It just seems unlike Holly. He must mean a lot to her, since she's been missing our catch-ups or leaving early to be with him. She's such a show-off usually.'

Izzy laughed. 'You have a point, there! But Holly would never do that. Be with a married man, I mean.'

Rachel didn't look too sure. 'You might be surprised, Izz. It's amazing what you find yourself doing when you think you love someone.' She shook her head. 'Ignore me. I'm being daft. Come on, let's get on with the wrapping up. Are you sure you don't mind me hiding all this stuff in your spare room?'

'Be my guest,' Izzy assured her. 'Although, you may struggle to fit it all in. I've already got an armchair balancing on top of the bed in there, so goodness knows where we're going to put all this.'

'We'll manage,' Rachel said. She drained her mug of hot chocolate and swallowed the last of her mince pie. 'Yummy. Thanks for that, Izz. Right, back to work!'

She dropped down onto the floor again and they spent an amiable hour or two, cutting wrapping paper, tearing off strips of tape, giggling helplessly at the mess they made of several of the presents, whose awkward shapes made a neat parcel impossible.

'Look at the state of that,' Rachel spluttered, holding up a colourfully-wrapped object that seemed to be more tape than paper. 'What a catastrophe.'

'Oh well, it all adds to the fun,' Izzy said.

It took them a good half hour to take all the parcels up to the spare room, and almost as long to find a way to stuff them all in without tearing, breaking or squashing them. Eventually, everything was crammed in and they thankfully shut the door on the chaotic scene within the room.

'Thanks ever so much, Izzy. I really appreciate this. You're a pal.'

'Not at all,' Izzy said, as they headed back downstairs. 'I've been glad of the distraction, to be honest.'

'I knew it!' Rachel threw herself onto the sofa and stared expectantly at her. 'I knew something was bothering you. What is it? Come on, you've heard my tales of woe enough in the past. You can tell me anything, you know.'

Izzy hesitated. She trusted Rachel, of course she did. But the thought of going over her own feelings of inadequacy again turned her stomach. Yes, Rachel knew she didn't want children, but even she would probably struggle to understand why Izzy felt unable to tell Ash that she loved him, too. Because, of course, she did love him. There was no doubt in her mind. That only made the situation even more impossible, though. Rachel loved Xander so much that, if he had really wanted a child of his own, Izzy was sure Rachel would have given in to please him. How could she be expected to accept that Izzy didn't feel able to do the same for Ash? And how could Izzy reveal how heartbroken she felt about the situation when, to other people, it must seem that there was an obvious solution? They would never be able to relate to her feelings.

'Izzy?'

Rachel's voice was gentle, and Izzy felt suddenly overwhelmed with it all. 'It's Anna,' she heard herself saying. 'Things are going from bad to worse.'

It wasn't entirely untrue, of course. Anna's attitude was very much playing on her mind, and her friend's new and flourishing relationship with Nell was hurting, no doubt about it. It wasn't Izzy's main problem, but it would ease Rachel's suspicions at least.

'What do you mean? What's wrong with Anna?'

'Nothing's wrong with Anna. She's perfectly happy.'

Rachel frowned, 'Is this the whole, *Anna wouldn't understand* thing again? I really do think you're reading too much into this, Izz.'

'I don't think I am.' Izzy swallowed, horrified to realise she had tears in her eyes. Where on earth had they come from? 'Something's come between us.'

'I'm sure nothing's come between you,' Rachel said softly.

'Oh yes it has. Nell, for starters.' There it was out. Now Rachel would know how pathetic and jealous Izzy really was. Great.

'Nell? What's Nell got to do with anything?'

And out it poured. All the little meetings between Anna and Nell, the pram shopping expedition, the trip to the hospital together, the meeting with the new GP, even the gushing over the baby clothes last night. Izzy poured it all out, while hating herself for every word. She loved Anna and she was very fond of Nell and, frankly, she was disgusted with herself for what she was saying but she couldn't seem to put the plug back in.

Rachel listened without interrupting and, when Izzy had finally finished, there was a long silence, broken only by the next carol on the CD starting. 'Away in a Manger'. *Well*, thought Izzy bitterly, *it would be, wouldn't it?*

'I can see this has really hurt you,' Rachel said slowly. 'And I do understand why. You and Anna have been friends for years, so of course you feel threatened. But you really shouldn't worry, you know. It will pass, I promise.'

'I don't see how,' Izzy sniffed. 'Anna clearly sees me as the equivalent of the Child Catcher from *Chitty, Chitty, Bang, Bang*. Nell's always been the motherly sort. She may hate weddings, but she's always wanted marriage and kids. She and Anna have a lot more in common than me and Anna have. I should have realised it before.'

She looked up, to see Rachel watching her with sympathy and — something else. 'What?'

Rachel looked as if she were about to say something, but she shook her head instead. 'Nothing. Just — don't let this upset you, Izz. Honestly, Anna's just at a funny time, right now, and Nell's — ' she shrugged, 'Nell's just got a kind heart and a maternal nature. You know that. I think you're being a bit over-sensitive because you've been through a lot with Matt. Your disagreement over having children broke up that relationship, so you're bound to be edgy.' She paused. 'Have you told Ash about not wanting kids?'

Izzy's head shot up. 'No! I mean, it's early days, isn't it? We've only been seeing each other for five minutes.'

Rachel looked awkward. 'I suppose so. It's just that, Ash is so — ' She smiled. 'Well, anyway, you know him best. Look, I'd better get off home or my mum will be sending out a search party. Are you sure you're going to be okay?'

'Of course I am! I'm going to have another hot chocolate, listen to a few more carols, then get an early night. Big day tomorrow.'

Rachel's face brightened. 'I know! I can't wait to see Sam. Xander's really excited, too. He's going to be home before lunch, so we can both make it to the play. Sam's so nervous, but he'll be okay, won't he?'

'He'll be fabulous,' Izzy said, smiling at the memory of Sam's dramatic death-bed performance. 'You're going to love this, I promise.'

'And you're going to be fine.' Rachel enfolded her in a hug. 'Trust Anna,' she said. 'She loves you like a sister, and that's not going to change. I'll see you tomorrow. Good luck!'

They headed into the hall and Izzy handed Rachel her coat. Buttoned up, hands in pockets, Rachel headed out into the freezing cold, and Izzy shut the door, glancing up at the mistletoe that hung above the door frame. She felt like pulling it down and hurling it in the fire. She would, after all, have no more use for mistletoe for a long, long time.

14

Mrs Morgan tutted in despair. 'Trust it to snow this week, of all weeks. The hall will be a mass of puddles with all the parents trampling it in, and the children are already over-excited before the play even starts. What is it with the wretched stuff that makes people go all silly?'

Ash didn't answer. He was too busy checking props. The TAs, helped by some of the handier parents, had done an amazing job with scenery and painted backdrops, and Mrs Morgan herself had done her fair share of sewing and altering costumes. It was a play that had gone as he wished — it involved as much of the school as was possible, from the little tots playing sleeping orphans to the older children, who were too cool to be on stage but were happy to act as ticket collectors and ushers for the evening.

The classroom next to the hall was a hive of activity, as pupils adjusted their dress, rehearsed their lines, or practised their singing. Next door, Jackson was warming up the piano. Row upon row of plastic chairs faced the stage. In a few minutes they would be occupied by excited and expectant parents.

Gracie was in the library, already in costume, being kept away from all the fluster and panic by her teaching assistant until it was time for her entrance.

Izzy was frantically hunting for Ebenezer Scrooge's night cap. Ash could hear her questioning Benjy about where he'd last had it, and Benjy replying that if he knew that he wouldn't need her help looking for it, would he?

Fair point, but now wasn't the time to get smart, Ash thought. Izzy was a nervous wreck and didn't need the extra stress.

Out of the corner of his eye, he spotted one of the four-year-olds, little Kara Edlinton, curled up with her blanket, sucking her thumb, the night cap dangling from her head. He went over to her and crouched down, removing it gently. 'Thanks, Kara, but that's needed now, okay?'

She nodded at him and he smiled. 'You're not going to sleep again, are you?'

She shook her head, grinning at him. 'Promise?'

'Promise,' she said, her blonde head bouncing enthusiastically.

Ash ruffled her hair and took the night cap over to Izzy.

'Oh, thank goodness for that!' she exclaimed, snatching it from him. 'Where was it?'

He nodded over at Kara. 'Little one had it,' he said. He watched as she handed it over to Benjy. 'Are you all right?'

'Fine. Why shouldn't I be? Only the biggest night of the school year and I'm responsible for it.'

He tried not to feel excluded by her statement. He'd thought it was a joint effort. Seemed he was wrong about that, as well as other things.

It had been a difficult two days. Excruciating. Izzy had used the frantic end-of-term activity as an excuse to avoid talking to him about their relationship. He cursed himself for telling her that he loved her. How could he be so stupid? It was far too soon to say such things, he realised that now. But they'd spent the weekend together, and, besides, he did love her. Desperately. Always had, if he was being honest with himself. He should have known it was too good to be true.

He mentally shook himself. Now wasn't the time to worry about their relationship. They had a play to direct, and dozens of young children who needed them to be focused and calm. That was all that mattered.

'The hall's nearly full.' Ash hadn't even noticed Jackson come in. 'You should hear the buzz next door. I'm getting quite nervous myself.'

'Great. Just what I needed to hear,

mate,' Ash said, smiling ruefully. 'You all set?'

Jackson flexed his fingers with a flourish. 'The maestro is at your command.'

'And the soundtrack's good to go?'

'Of course it is. Come on, Ash, we've done this before, many times. Stop worrying.'

'Can't help it.'

'Sure you can. It's always gone perfectly in the past. What's so different this time?'

Ash gave him a meaningful look. 'This time, I told my girlfriend I loved her, and she couldn't say it back.'

Jackson winced. 'Ouch.' He patted Ash on the shoulder. 'Now's not the time, mate.'

'That's what *she* said.' Ash tutted. 'You're right. Let's focus on the play. That's what really matters right now.'

'Good man.' Jackson rubbed his bearded chin thoughtfully. 'Before you go into the hall, though, maybe there's something I should warn you about, given what you've just told me.'

Ash groaned. 'What? Don't tell me, the piano needs tuning. The scenery's fallen down. The CD player's broken.'

'Nothing like that. It's the blond Adonis. He's sitting at the back of the hall.'

'What?' Ash gaped at him. 'Matt Jones? You're sure?'

'You can't miss him, can you? You said it yourself. Looks like a rugby player.'

'What's he doing here?' Ash was furious. 'He's got no right.'

'Seems little Kara Edlinton is his niece,' Jackson said. At Ash's raised eyebrow he added, 'I thought the same as you. He had no right. So, I checked, and he's here with his sister and they have tickets so . . . Sorry, mate.'

And just why, thought Ash, would Matt Jones turn up to watch his niece in her school play? Surely, he had better things to do with his time? Rugby matches to play, Mr Universe contests to win, that sort of thing.

Ash's jaw tightened. He'd come to

see Izzy, hadn't he? No doubt about it. And he had an awful feeling he knew why.

★   ★   ★

Izzy was just beginning to relax. So far, so good.

There had been a couple of worrying moments, like when Noah had accidentally called the boy playing Fagin by his real name, Josh, and when Sara had forgotten one of her lines and had been nudged by a dramatic stage whisper from Theo, who was playing the ghost of her husband, Bob Cratchitt, much to the amusement of the audience.

Overall, though, things were going well. Gracie had held the audience spellbound as she sang 'A Cruel Heart' then led the choir in 'God Rest Ye Merry Gentlemen', and Izzy saw Anna's tear-streaked face as she and Connor sat, enthralled by her performance.

All the children, it seemed, were thoroughly enjoying themselves. A glance through the curtains at the parents showed that they, too, were clearly having a great time. She wished she could feel as happy.

Every now and then she caught a glimpse of Ash, standing at the other side of the stage, whispering instructions to a child or adjusting a costume, or just offering reassurance, no doubt. A couple of times he'd looked across at her and their eyes had met briefly, before one or other of them looked hastily away.

She knew she'd hurt him, and it broke her heart. But he had no idea how much pain *she* was feeling, or how she was doing her level best to make this as easy for him as she could. It was for his own good, after all.

Watching his interactions with the children that afternoon, seeing how they flocked around him, hanging on his every word, responding to his calm reassurances and encouraging praise, she could see it so clearly. He was meant to be a dad and she'd bet anything that he couldn't wait for the great day when that finally happened. Maybe, just maybe, he would sacrifice his dreams to be with her, but she wouldn't allow it. He deserved to be a father, perhaps more than any man she knew.

As the last notes of 'Away in a Manger' died away, Izzy blinked away the tears and pulled herself together. A quick glance into the audience made her smile, as she saw the mums — and even a few dads — furtively mopping away tears. She'd known that would get them. It never failed. She was relieved that little Kara had managed to stay awake. She seemed quite lively, and even gave a cheeky little wave as the curtains closed on the orphanage scene.

'Where's Abel?' she said, looking around frantically for the boy who was playing the Ghost of Christmas Yet to Come. He shuffled forwards, fastening the cord of his black, hooded dressing gown. It was one of his father's cast-offs and Izzy hoped the audience wouldn't notice the bare patch in the fleece where, just a few days ago, a Liverpool Football Club badge had nestled. 'All set?'

He nodded, supremely confident in the role. Izzy smiled at him, remembering how sullen and awkward he could be in class. She hadn't had a minute's trouble from him during rehearsals. He'd thrown himself into the part with relish. Ash had told her he would.

As the Ghost of Christmas Yet to Come took Scrooge to the orphanage of the future, revealing a sobbing Mrs Cratchitt, a desolate Fagin, and weeping orphans mourning Oliver's loss, she contemplated her own future and the prospect of losing Ash.

Funny, she thought, how just the idea of it was hurting her more than the actual break-up with Matt had done. She'd honestly thought she loved Matt but being with Ash had shown her that she hadn't. Not really. Her relationship with him hadn't even scratched the surface, whereas with Ash she felt she'd discovered something startlingly new and precious. How was she going to cope without him?

It was Sam's turn to star, and Izzy concentrated hard as he performed his dramatic death bed scene. She peered into the audience, seeking Rachel. She was sitting in the middle of the hall, eyes fixed on the stage. Izzy knew that Xander was there, somewhere, too. He'd decided to sneak in apart from Rachel. Too many of the parents knew they were a couple and would assume he'd be sitting with her and Xander didn't want the kids competing with him for attention.

He wasn't being vain. It was a sad fact that, when he'd turned up for sports day in July, most of the mothers hadn't even noticed their children's efforts, being too busy gaping at the television star in their midst. Xander was determined it wouldn't happen this time. He'd waited until Rachel had time to take her seat, then had crept in to sit at the back, a black woolly hat hiding his blond hair, a pair of fake glasses hopefully distracting attention from those famous blue eyes. Spotting him, Izzy saw the clear pride in his face as he watched Sam gasp his last. You'd never know Xander wasn't his real father if you were judging it by that expression, she thought.

Her eyes narrowed suddenly. Was that — *Matt?* What was he doing here? She supposed he must have come to see Kara, although she didn't have him down as the school play type. Then again, children were clearly more important to him than she'd realised. Their break-up was proof of that.

She forced herself to focus on the play. Scrooge was witnessing his own death, and Benjy was doing a great job of looking appalled as Fagin and Dodger helped themselves to his belongings. They cackled at their good fortune that no one cared what happened to Ebenezer, before launching into the song 'It's a Grand Day for Some' as they gleefully examined his clothes, paintings and orna-ments — most of which had come from charity shops or parents who wanted rid of the tat, anyway, but still.

Izzy shivered. Who would care for her when she died, she wondered suddenly. Her parents would be gone, she had no brothers or sisters, and it seemed she was doomed to spend the rest of her life alone. Maybe, just maybe, she should think again. Could she — should she — have a child, after all? How much easier it would be to give Ash what he wanted, needed, and keep him in her life. Surely, it was worth considering, at least?

She wrapped her arms around herself, nodding encouragingly as the children filed onstage for the final scene.

Scrooge had, thankfully, realised the error of his ways. He had sent Fagin across London to inform Oliver's grandfather of the existence of his grandson, and he'd organised a Christmas feast for the orphans, promising Mrs Cratchitt that, from now on, the children would be warm, well-fed, well-clothed, and would receive an education that would equip them for a secure adulthood.

Oliver's grandfather arrived, over-come with joy to discover his lost daughter's child, and promised that he would receive the best medical care and would live a long and happy life under his roof. Then the whole cast gathered together on stage and the children gave a heartfelt and moving rendition of 'O Little Town of Bethlehem' before the final curtain fell.

Across the stage, Izzy's eyes met Ash's and this time neither of them looked away. He smiled at her and gave her a thumbs up, and she nodded, smiling back. They'd done it. Whatever happened now, they'd achieved what they'd set out to do. This was a play that Bramblewick Primary School could remember with pride for a long time to come.

Which was, more-or-less, what Mrs Morgan said, as she went on stage to address the parents. She thanked them for their support and encouragement, and thanked all the children for taking part, whether that was on stage or behind the scenes. She got the whole audience to applaud the teachers and TAs who had helped, and gave a special mention to Jackson Wade, who stepped out from behind the piano and took a bow, earning himself a huge cheer.

Mrs Morgan held up her hands, calming everyone down. 'Finally,' she said, 'I'd like to give an extra special thanks to the two people without whom this play could never have happened. Ladies and gentlemen, boys and girls, please give a huge round of applause to our directors, Miss Clark and Mr Uttridge.'

The whole hall seemed to erupt with cheers and the sound of clapping, as Ash and Izzy stepped forward, each clearly as embarrassed as the other. Mrs Morgan gave them both a hug and told them to take a bow. Ash hesitated, then he took hold of Izzy's hand and they bowed low in a gesture worthy of Oscar winners.

Izzy heard whistling, though she wasn't sure where it was coming from and didn't dare look too closely. She was trying to hold it together, standing there, Ash's hand clasping hers tightly, as if he never wanted to let it go.

Suddenly the stage was invaded, as the whole cast seemed to swarm towards them. Izzy and Ash were pulled apart, enveloped in hugs, and the applause from the audience was drowned out by the squeals of joy and excitement from the children. Izzy laughed and hugged them back, glancing over at Ash. The joy seemed to die within her as she saw his expression. His eyes were sparkling, and his whole face was alight with pleasure. The kids were gazing up at him adoringly.

She couldn't bear the thought of letting him go but seeing him surrounded by all those youngsters who clearly thought the world of him, she knew she couldn't deprive him of a child of his own.

She had to make a choice, and decision time had arrived.

15

Izzy tapped the keypad of her phone, barely able to see what she was writing, her eyes were so blurred with tears.

WILL BE JOINING YOU IN SPAIN FOR CHRISTMAS. TEXT YOU TOMORROW WITH FLIGHT DETAILS. LOVE YOU BOTH. XX

She pressed send before she could change her mind then gulped down the rest of her wine. It was a good job, she thought dully, that she only had half a bottle in the fridge. If she'd had more, she'd have been in serious danger of downing the lot, and that wouldn't do her any good. Luckily, she hadn't done her Christmas grocery shop yet. She'd been planning to do that on Saturday, hopefully with Ash.

She dropped her phone and leaned back in the chair, closing her eyes. She'd had it all planned. Christmas shopping on the Saturday, Ash staying overnight, then the carol service on the Sunday at St Benedict's — an annual tradition in Bramblewick. It would have been even more special this year, because Sunday was Christmas Eve, and maybe she and Ash could have spent the big day together, too. He hadn't mentioned having other plans. Maybe he'd been waiting for her to suggest something. Maybe . . .

She sat up straight, slamming the glass down on the occasional table at the side of her chair. She couldn't do this. How could she fly off to Spain to join her parents, pretend to be happy, to be in the Christmas mood, when she felt so low? Yet, how could she stay in the village, feeling as miserable as this? Everything that *could* go wrong *had* gone wrong, and Izzy didn't know what to do any more.

She'd considered it, she really had. Having a baby for Ash's sake. For a brief moment, it had seemed like a small sacrifice to make. She would do anything to keep him — no, *almost* anything.

The limitations had only been confirmed when she was approached by Matt the moment she left the stage.

He'd pulled her into a hug as if they were best friends, rather than two people who'd had no contact whatsoever for over three months. 'Izzy, you look fantastic! Congratulations. Great job with the play.'

Izzy had given him a tight smile. 'Thanks. Kara did really well.'

'What? Oh, yes, yes, she did. Izz, can we go somewhere and talk?'

Izzy had glanced around, seeing Ash surrounded by grateful and gushing parents. She tucked her hair behind her ears and shrugged. 'What is there to talk about?'

'But that's just it, there's a lot to talk about. I have something I need to tell you, Izzy.'

As she looked at him doubtfully, he said, 'Please. It's important.'

Sighing, she'd nodded and led him

out of the hall, taking him to an empty classroom a few doors down the corridor. 'I can't be long,' she told him. 'I've got to help with the children. I can't leave all the clearing up and calming down to the other members of staff. I'm the director. It's my responsibility.'

'Izzy.' He said her name softly and she peered at him, feeling a bit bewildered.

'What's going on, Matt?'

'You and me. I want us to have another chance, Izz. I want us to get back together.'

Izzy laughed, though she felt far from amused. 'Are you crazy? We've said all we had to say about that subject, haven't we? I think they call it irreconcilable differences.'

'But that's just it. Maybe we can reconcile them.'

Izzy narrowed her eyes. 'What are you talking about, Matt? I told you — '

'That you don't want children. I know. I remember. But maybe that's something I'm willing to compromise on. Look,' he said hurriedly as she opened her mouth to protest, 'I know what I said, but I've had a lot of time to think about it. The truth is, I always wanted children, but I think — I know — that if it's a choice, I want you more. I love you, Izzy. I want our relationship to work, and if that means giving up on having a family then — ' he took a deep breath, ' — then I'll do it.'

Izzy stared at him, hardly able to believe what she'd heard. All the arguments they'd had, all the tears she'd shed, his impassioned pleas to her to reconsider, her sobbing assurances that she knew what she was saying and there was no way she could change her mind, all flooded back to her. She gazed into the navy-blue depths of his eyes. There were no gold flecks to be seen. She sank into one of the chairs and shook her head, feeling dazed.

'I'm sorry, Matt. It would never work.'

'But it would.' He pulled up a chair

and sat beside her, looking completely ridiculous — his large frame dwarfing the tiny plastic construction. 'Look, this is my choice to make, surely? If I'm willing to give up having kids to be with you, then that's my decision, isn't it? And I've made it. We were good together, we can't just walk away over something that may never have happened anyway. I might not be able to have children, have you thought of that? Or you might not. No one knows. So, surely, we should base our future on what we know for certain, and what I know for certain is that I want to be with you.'

Izzy reached out a hand and took hold of his. 'Oh, Matt, I'm so sorry. The truth is, children or no children, I don't want to be with you anymore. Our relationship is over. It would never work anyway. You say you're willing to give up having a family, but how do you know that, one day, you won't bitterly regret that and hold me responsible?' She squeezed his hand, her heart heavy.

'In just the same way that, if I gave in and had a child for your sake, I might well regret that. And it wouldn't just be me who suffered the consequences of that mistake. It would be a poor innocent child.'

She realised it was what she'd known all along, even as she'd tried to convince herself that she could push her feelings to one side to keep Ash. No child deserved that fate. It would be cruel to everyone concerned.

Matt looked down at his hand, held in hers. 'You really mean it, don't you? No going back.'

'I'm sorry,' she told him, meaning it. 'You meant the world to me, you really did, but it's over.'

He removed his hand from her grasp and gave a short laugh. 'I kind of knew you were going to say that,' he admitted, gazing up at her with sad eyes. 'I figured it had to be worth one last shot, though.'

'One day,' she promised him, 'you're going to thank me for this.'

'I'll take your word for that,' he said, struggling to his feet. 'I'd better go and find my sister.' He hesitated, then hugged her again. 'Take care of yourself, Izzy. Merry Christmas.'

Izzy had held him tightly. 'Merry Christmas, Matt.'

He'd nodded, then let her go, and she'd watched as he left the classroom, closing the door behind him, and closing the book, finally, on their relationship.

Izzy wasn't sure how she'd got through the rest of the working day but, somehow, she'd finally made it home to her refuge at Rose Cottage. If only she could switch off her mind. She was exhausted. Misery could really wear you out.

She stood up and wandered over to the Christmas tree, her fingers idly playing with one of the baubles hanging from its branches: a little silver cherub that had been in the family since she was a little girl. Her mother had bought it for her when she was about four and had made a huge deal of taking it out of its tissue paper wrapping every year. She'd made a big deal of Christmas, full stop, making sure that Izzy had everything she wanted, and turning the festive season into a time of wonder and delight. She was a good mother and Izzy knew she was lucky to have her.

Why, she wondered, didn't she have those maternal feelings? Why did she feel no desire to have a baby when it seemed to be what every other woman wanted? She loved babies, she really did — when they were someone else's. She was quite happy to coo over them and hold them in her arms and cuddle them, but only because she knew she could hand them back whenever she chose. Having one of her own simply wasn't an option.

No wonder her mum couldn't understand. No wonder Anna thought she was odd and had turned to Nell instead.

Well, whatever was wrong with her, at least she was brave enough to admit it and stand by her decision.

After Matt had left, Izzy had waited a moment or two, regaining her composure, then had headed back to the hall to begin the clearing up process. Surrounded by excited children, it had been very easy to steer clear of Ash, and she'd worked deftly and quickly, ensuring the costumes were packed away, props sorted, scenery dismantled, and children taken back to their classrooms in time for the final bell. After that, she'd avoided the staff room, where she knew her colleagues would be gathering to celebrate and had instead rushed straight home.

She would tell Ash the truth, she really would. But not today. She couldn't face it. Maybe, she thought bleakly, she would wait until after Christmas. Tell him when she got home from Spain. She just had to avoid him for two more days and then term would be over, and she could rush off to the airport. Could she be that cruel? That cowardly?

At a knock on the door, Izzy felt her

heart somersault in fear. It had to be Ash. How could she face him? She wasn't ready, she thought, panicked. She didn't know what to tell him. Taking a deep breath, she steadied herself and headed to the door, pulling it open with grim fortitude.

But it wasn't Ash. It was Anna. And, judging by her expression, she clearly had plenty to say to her.

★　★　★

Izzy's heart seemed to leap into her mouth. 'Anna! What are you doing here?' She peered round. 'Are you on your own?'

'I am. Connor's taken Gracie to the station to collect Dottie, so I thought I'd take the opportunity to have a little word in your shell-like, if that's okay with you?'

Her tone brooked no arguments and Izzy knew she was already defeated. 'You'd better come in,' she said, reluctantly holding open the door so that Anna could squeeze past. 'Go through to the living room,' she said. 'Warm yourself up.'

Anna did so, after stamping her feet on the doormat to dislodge all the loose snow. Izzy took a deep breath and shut the door, glancing up at the mistletoe as she did so. A lump lodged in her throat, and she steadied herself before following her friend into the room.

'Tea? Coffee?'

Anna shook her head. 'No thanks, Izz. I'm not stopping long. I'm worn out, to be honest, and I've got awful backache.' She smiled. 'Probably from sitting on that tiny chair watching the play. Congratulations, by the way. What a triumph.'

'You enjoyed it?' Izzy began to relax. 'I'm so glad. Wasn't Gracie wonderful? The star of the show.'

'Well, one of them,' Anna acknowledged. 'They were all brilliant. The whole play was fantastic. We loved it and, judging by the audience's reaction, we weren't the only ones.'

'I know! All that applause and those

cheers. We weren't expecting all that, you know. Such a relief.'

'Hmm.' Anna leaned back in her chair. 'Which makes it even stranger that you rushed off afterwards. We saw Ash and he looked devastated. What's going on, Izzy?'

Izzy gulped. 'I don't know what you mean.'

'Yes, you do. He was looking for you and you'd disappeared. He was desolate, and it doesn't take a genius to work out that something's gone badly wrong. This should have been the best afternoon of your professional life, and of his, yet he looked like he'd just been sacked, and you'd run off as if you were ashamed of the play or something. We congratulated him, me and Connor, told him how wonderful *A Twisted Christmas* was and how well you'd both done. You know what? He looked as miserable as sin. And I knew — I just knew — that he was dying to ask me about you or tell me something. But, of course, he couldn't because he was still dealing with parents and children and other members of staff, whereas you — where the hell were you, Izzy?'

'Matt showed up.' Izzy thought she'd better speak up or she might never get a word in edgeways.

'Matt? I thought I saw him, but Connor said I must have been imagining it. What did he want?' She stared at Izzy, aghast. 'You're not getting back with him!'

'Don't say it like that,' Izzy protested. 'Anyway, I thought you liked Matt.'

'I did. I do.' Anna ran a hand through her hair, looking bewildered. 'He's a nice guy, of course he is, but he's not — well, Ash. And besides, I thought you and he were over because of — well, you know.'

Izzy scowled. 'You can say it, you know. Because I don't want children, and he does. It's not catching if you put it into words.'

Anna frowned. 'What are you talking about?'

'Oh, don't deny it. I know how you feel about the whole situation!'

'What situation?'

'Me not wanting kids. I'm some sort of heartless freak in your eyes, Anna, and I'm very well aware of the fact, thanks very much.'

Anna's mouth dropped open. 'I have never, ever said that! I never thought it for one second. Where on earth did you get that idea?'

'It doesn't matter. The point is, I'm not getting back with Matt, and I'm not going to be with Ash for much longer, anyway, so there you go.'

'I don't understand.' Anna leaned forward and reached for Izzy's hand. 'What's going on, Izzy? Why won't you be with Ash for much longer? And what did Matt want?'

Izzy sat on the sofa, folding her legs under her and wondering where to start. 'Matt wanted us to have another chance,' she said eventually. 'He said he loves me enough to sacrifice having a family and wanted me to take him back.'

Anna's eyes widened. 'Wow! That's

some sacrifice. And what did you say?'

'What do you think I said? I told him it would never work. I couldn't ask him to give up on having children when I know how important it is to him. Besides, the truth is, I've realised I never loved Matt in the same way I love Ash, so it would be stupid and cruel to take him back now.'

'You do love Ash then? I knew it. And you do know he loves you, don't you? Honestly, Izz, I could read it all over his face. He's so miserable, not knowing what he's done wrong and — '

'He told me he loves me,' Izzy burst out. 'That's what he's done wrong.'

'But — but you love him! You've just said so. Oh!' Anna threw up her hands in despair. 'You've completely lost me.'

'Ash loves me, and I love him, but I could never tell him that because, what's the use? You saw him today. You saw the way he was with the children, and how they flock around him so adoringly. He's a born father, no doubt about it. How can I stop him from becoming one? And I won't change my mind about having children, before you start. I can't do it, it just isn't me and it wouldn't be fair to any of us if I gave in to keep him. So, what's the use? It's over. It has to be.'

Anna surveyed her. 'And Ash has told you that, has he? That he's desperate to be a father?'

'He doesn't have to, does he?'

'Well, actually, I think he does, yes. You're making massive assumptions there. Just because he's good with kids, doesn't mean he wants some of his own. You made that point about yourself, very forcefully as I recall, not that long ago. Why should it be true of you and not of him?'

'Because — because he's exceptional around them.' Izzy floundered. 'You can just see it in his face.'

'Have you even told him that you don't want kids?' Anna demanded.

'Of course I haven't!'

'Why on earth not?'

'Because funnily enough, I didn't

want to lose him, and we all know that people who don't want kids are evil trolls, so he's bound to dump me the minute he finds out.'

'Evil trolls? Izzy, what on earth are you talking about? Seriously, I'm getting worried about you.'

'Really?' Izzy could feel her emotions getting rapidly out of control. It felt as if she had a huge block of concrete sitting in her chest, and tears were only seconds away. 'Well, I thought you'd be too busy thinking about Nell to spare a thought for me.'

'Nell?' Anna bit her lip. 'Is that what this has all been about? You're jealous of Nell?'

Izzy had never wanted to disappear through a hole in the ground more than she did at that moment. 'Not jealous,' she managed eventually. 'Hurt. Yes, hurt,' she repeated defiantly. 'We were best friends, Anna, and the moment you found out I didn't want kids you dumped me for Nell.'

'Who on earth says I dumped you?'

Anna sounded genuinely baffled.

'You took Nell pram shopping, she went to the hospital appointment with you, all those flipping baby clothes she bought for you as if she was your best pal from way back. I should have gone pram shopping with you. I should have been at the hospital appointment. I should be the one buying the baby presents! We've been best friends since we were five years old and now it's like I'm not fit for purpose any more. Just because I told you I didn't want kids doesn't change who I am, you know. I've never wanted kids, but you liked me before you knew that. I just think — '

'You don't think at all,' Anna rebuked her. 'You just made yet more assumptions. I've never for a moment thought any less of you for not wanting to become a mother. Why would I? It doesn't change you, as you say, and it doesn't change anything between us. You've just decided that *I've* changed and it's unfair of you. I thought you knew me better than that.'

'So did I,' Izzy muttered.

'You really think it matters to me that much? It doesn't matter to me at all! I only care that you're happy, Izz, and you're not happy. You love Ash and he loves you. Why aren't you with him right now?'

'I've just told you why!'

'Yes, you have! Because you're making huge assumptions about him, as well as about me. Why don't you go to his place and tell him the truth? It's cruel to leave him wondering what he did wrong when all he did was tell you how he felt about you.'

Izzy shook her head. 'I can't. I just have to get through the next couple of days and then I'm flying off to Spain to spend Christmas with my parents. All this stuff can wait until I get back.'

'Spain! Since when?'

Izzy hung her head and Anna tutted. 'So, you fly off to Spain and leave Ash to have a miserable Christmas alone in Helmston, wondering what the hell went wrong.'

'I'll be miserable, too!' Izzy protested, stung. It wasn't as if she'd be downing sangria and dancing the flamenco with joy, was it? She'd be having a Christmas from hell, quite frankly, trying to keep up some semblance of merriment for her parents' sake when, all the time, she'd be wanting to curl up into a ball and pretend Christmas wasn't even happening.

'Great. So, there'll be two miserable people, not one. And all because you haven't got the courage to tell him the truth.' Anna folded her arms over her bump. 'I honestly can't believe you, Izz. How can you be this cruel?'

'I'm not being cruel,' Izzy said.

'Yes you are. You're not telling him what's going on and he deserves the truth. He deserves to have his say. At least give him the chance to share his views with you. You're doing to him what you've been doing to me. Putting your own interpretation on things and punishing him for something he hasn't even done. You need to stop being so gutless and face up to things.'

Izzy wanted to argue back but she found the words had died in her throat. Anna was right, she realised. She wasn't giving Ash the opportunity to have a grown-up conversation about their future. He deserved, at least, to know why they could never work. 'I need to go to his flat,' she said. 'I'm sorry, Anna, about everything.'

Anna waved her arm in the air. 'Forget it,' she said. 'Just go to Helmston and sort this out.' She pulled herself to her feet and winced.

'You okay?' Izzy asked anxiously, hurrying over to her side.

'Fine. Just my back. Wretched school chairs.' Anna gave her a feeble smile. 'So, you'll go and see him? Tonight?'

Izzy nodded. 'I promise. As soon as you've gone.'

'Then I'm off home right now,' Anna said. She put her arms around Izzy. 'As if anyone could ever take your place, you daft ha'porth. You're my best friend. Always have been. Always will be.'

Izzy still couldn't fathom what was going on with Nell but, for now, Anna's words were comfort enough. She had to focus on what was important and, right now, nothing was more important than explaining the truth to Ash and giving him the chance to walk away. Letting him be the one to break off their relationship was the very least she could do for him. It was *all* she could do for him.

16

The faint hum from the electric stove was getting on Ash's nerves. He sat glaring at it for a moment or two, before giving up and pulling out the plug with more force than was strictly necessary. He glanced around the flat, seeing only the tacky gaudiness of the Christmas tree and the trimmings that adorned the ceiling and walls. As if they made any difference to this place, for goodness sake. He must have been mad, thinking he could inject some cheer into this soulless box.

He hesitated for a moment, then strode into the hallway, wrenching open the door of the cupboard and pulling out his stepladder. Dragging it back into the living room, he climbed the steps and reached for the corner of the silver and red foil garland. With a ferocious tug, the garland tore, and the end drooped aimlessly before him, while the faint ping from a vase on the sideboard told him that the drawing pin had landed. He climbed down, moved the stepladder to the other end of the garland and repeated the process.

Ten minutes later, all the trimmings were down and only the Christmas tree remained. Ash folded up the ladder and put it back in the cupboard before standing before the tree, considering. Should he take that down, as well? It would be a bleak Christmas without it, but then again, it was going to be a bleak Christmas anyway. Mind made up, he reached up, removed the fairy from the top and dropped it onto the sofa. Unplugging the lights, he began to unwind them, almost tugging at them as they snagged on branches, rattling the baubles, causing many of them to drop to the floor. He should have removed the baubles first, of course, but it was done now. He didn't really care. So what if some of them broke? They were cheap market tat. Replaceable. Like him.

He'd seen her — or rather, he'd seen them. Through the glass panel in the door of the classroom. Izzy and Mr Universe. Hugging tightly, as if they'd never been apart. Clearly, they were back together. No wonder she'd rushed off after the play was over. No wonder she hadn't stuck around to celebrate. He wondered wretchedly how long their reconciliation had been on the cards. It explained why she'd been avoiding him for days at school, anyway. He'd assumed it was because he'd told her he loved her. How she must have laughed at that. Had she told Matt? Had they both been laughing at him?

He didn't want to believe it of her. Izzy had a good heart, he was sure of it. But then, what did he know of human nature? Very little, obviously. He'd been sure that Izzy felt the same way about him as he did about her — especially after their magical weekend together. Clearly, he'd been very wrong about that. When he'd revealed the depths of his feelings to her she'd run a mile

— straight back into the arms of Matt Jones. Well, it was done, and he just had to snap out of it. He'd done it before, after all.

The doorbell rang, and Ash groaned inwardly. Great. Probably Jackson come to cheer him up with bottles of Lusty Tup and a tin full of mince pies. It wouldn't work. And, of course, now he'd get the whole lecture about letting his emotions get the better of him, and he could hardly deny it because the wrecked tree and a floor strewn with snapped garlands were proof that he had, indeed, succumbed.

'Okay, okay, keep your hair on.' He muttered to himself as the doorbell rang again. *Give me a chance*, he thought. Should he tidy away the garlands first, at least? The doorbell rang again, twice this time. Jackson was persistent if nothing else. He'd just have to face up to his rash actions then. Anything to shut that wretched doorbell up, he thought, as it rang yet again.

He marched into the hall, glaring at

the mistletoe that he'd placed above the door. Dratted stuff. That would be the next thing to hit the bin, he decided, throwing open the door as he prepared to launch into a verbal attack about people who abused doorbells in such a reckless fashion.

His protests died in his throat and he gaped at Izzy as she stood in the hall outside, her face pale, her brown eyes large and nervous as she stared back at him.

'Izzy.' He'd managed that much, at least. 'I — I wasn't expecting to see you. I mean — '

'I can imagine.' She shrugged. 'Am I allowed to come in?'

He blinked, feeling stupid. 'Of course. Yes, come in.' Although, even as he said it, he wondered why. Why would he want her to come in and see how much their tattered relationship had affected his mood? Why would he invite her to put the final nail in the coffin of their romance? Because, no doubt, it was what she'd come to do. To tell him all about her and Matt and to say how sorry she was that it hadn't worked out, but she just couldn't help herself. It had always been Matt. It always would be.

And he could relate to that because, for him, it had always been Izzy. Since the day he'd walked into the staff room at Bramblewick Primary and seen her sitting in a chair, clutching a Harry Potter mug, and giggling like mad with another teacher over some article in a magazine they were flicking through, it had been her. She'd looked up as Mrs Morgan introduced him, and her smile had lit up her whole face. And it had lit something within him, too, something that he thought had died forever after his broken engagement. He couldn't blame Izzy for going back to Matt if that's how she felt about him. There always had to be a loser in any love triangle, and it was just too bad that, this time, it was him.

Izzy had entered the living room and she stopped dead in front of him. 'What happened?' she cried. 'Your tree. The decorations!'

She'd helped him put them all up, he remembered, that day after they met in Helmston Market. How could she not realise what had happened?

She turned to look at him and he knew, suddenly, that she had realised. 'Oh, Ash,' she murmured. 'I'm so sorry.'

He gulped down the pain, trying hard not to give in to the tears that were threatening. 'Yeah, well,' he said, clearing his throat, 'it's done now.'

'I never meant to hurt you,' she whispered. 'I swear I didn't. I — '

'Look, Izz, can we just cut to the chase and get it over with?' Ash didn't think he could stand any prolonged explanations. 'It's okay. I saw you both. You and Matt hugging in the classroom. I get it, okay? I — I wish you luck, I really do.'

Her eyes widened, and she shook her head frantically. 'No, no you've got it all wrong. I'm not back with Matt!'

The ground seemed to lurch beneath his feet and he sank onto the sofa. 'You're not?'

'No. Hell, no!' She sat beside him and reached for his hand. 'Oh, Ash, is that what you thought? I'm so sorry.'

'Well, you weren't around to ask,' he pointed out.

'I know. I got scared. I was a coward. I should have told you — ' She sighed. 'This is so hard.'

'What did Matt want? And why was he hugging you?'

'We were saying goodbye. Matt — he wanted another chance. He wanted us to make a go of it, but I said no. It could never work. There were good, solid reasons for our break-up, Ash, and no coming back from them.'

'You don't have to tell me,' he said, hoping she would. He wasn't sure what to think any more. If she wasn't back with Matt, had she come to tell him she and Ash were still together after all?

'I do have to tell you,' she said softly, and he heard the regret in her voice and his heart sank. 'Because, the truth is, the reason Matt and I can't be together is the same reason that you and I can't be together.'

He squeezed her hand, hanging onto her for grim death. 'Don't say that, Izz. Whatever it is — '

'Please, Ash, let me finish.' Her voice was shaky, and he realised how hard this was for her. Whatever the problem, it was obviously huge. Insurmountable.

'Go on,' he said, feeling helpless.

'I decided, a long, long time ago that I never wanted children.'

Ash nodded. 'Yeah, I know. And?'

Izzy dropped his hand and stared at him. 'Pardon?'

'I know. You told me that ages ago. But what's that got to do with — ' A thought occurred to him suddenly and he felt a bubbling surge of hope. 'Izzy! Is that the problem? Is that what you needed to tell me?'

She nodded, seeming struck dumb by his response.

'But don't you remember?' He shook

his head impatiently. 'Of course you don't. You didn't even remember our kiss and that was the same night. We went out to the pub in Whitby, remember I told you? And we had a long chat, putting the world to rights over a few drinks. And during that chat, you told me you didn't want children, and I said — '

'What? What did you say?' Izzy seemed to be holding her breath.

'I said that I understood that completely, because I'd never wanted them either.'

Izzy seemed to be in shock. She clutched at his arm, as if for support. 'Ash, don't mess around with this, please. You have to tell me the truth. What did you really say?'

'I've just told you. You were upset because you and your mum had just had a bit of an argument about it on the phone. You couldn't believe that she didn't see it from your point of view and I said to you I totally got it because I'd had the same argument with my parents. They thought I was weird. Still do, actually, although they're coming to terms with it now, and since my brother's made them grandparents they've eased off on me. Izz, are you okay?'

'You don't want kids? But, but you're so good with them!' Izzy was in tears and Ash put his arm around her. 'How can someone like you not want them? You're the best teacher I've ever seen.'

'Well, thank you,' Ash said, rather perplexed. 'I could say the same to you. But that's my job, Izzy, and I love it. Don't get me wrong about that. I love being around the kids, and I love helping them to become the people I know they're capable of being. Doesn't mean I have any desire to have any of my own, does it? You should know that.'

'You're not just saying this?'

He took both her hands in his. 'Izzy, do you remember I told you about my broken engagement? Well, I made the mistake of asking her to marry me and then discussing the children issue. Turned out, she had plans for a mini football team. That's why our engagement only lasted seven hours. I swear to you, I'm not making this up.' As she let out a broken sob, he pulled her to him. 'Oh, Izzy, is that what this has all been about?'

'I thought you'd break up with me when you found out,' she said through her tears. 'I thought you'd think I was a selfish freak. I didn't think you'd understand, and I was so sure you'd want kids that I couldn't bear to tell you and lose you. I hung on as long as I could, but then you said you loved me, and I knew I had to be honest because — because I love you, too, you see. So much.'

'You do?' Ash could barely see her for his own tears. 'Really?'

'Really.'

Ash watched her for a moment, then he stood up. 'Wait right there,' he instructed.

She watched him, anxiety written across her face, as he returned and stood before her. 'Since it's Christmas, I think we should do this in proper festive fashion,' he told her, holding up the mistletoe that he'd just removed from above his front door. He saw the smile light up her face in that way that he so loved, and his heart leapt as she jumped up and put her arms around him. The mistletoe didn't stay above them for long. In the passion of their kiss, his arm dropped and wrapped around her and, eventually, the mistletoe fell to the ground forgotten. It didn't really matter. It had, after all, served its purpose.

They might have stood there forever if not for the persistent ringing of the mobile phone in Izzy's pocket.

'Just leave it,' he murmured, his lips against hers, and Izzy didn't seem in any mood to disagree.

When the caller rang for the third time, though, they admitted defeat and pulled apart. Izzy took out her phone and answered it, and Ash watched, his impatience turning to anxiety as he saw the expression on her face.

'Who was it?' he asked, as she shoved the phone back in her pocket.

'Connor,' she said. 'Anna's in hospital, and this time it's the real deal.'

'You have to go,' he said, trying to be generous. 'Anna needs you.'

'And I need you,' she told him, grabbing his hand. 'I'm going to the hospital, but you're coming with me. I'm not letting you out of my sight for a minute, sweetheart.'

Ash grinned and nodded. He wasn't going to argue. He was never going to let Izzy go again.

17

Chestnut House seemed full to bursting. Gracie and Sam were sitting at the kitchen table with Dottie, who was asking them lots of questions about *A Twisted Christmas* and seemed genuinely absorbed in hearing all about it. Ash, Xander and Connor were on kettle duty, making cups of tea on a loop and hunting around for biscuits. In the living room, Anna sat cradling her not-so-tiny baby, while Holly, Izzy and Rachel gazed adoringly at them and bombarded the new mum with endless questions.

'But nine pounds three!' Holly looked aghast. 'How on earth did you fit her in?'

'Er, did you see the size of that bump?' Izzy said, laughing. 'I'm only surprised she wasn't a ten-pounder.'

Anna pulled a face. 'I know! And I've still got a bump, too. I was expecting it to have gone by now.'

'You must be joking.' Rachel gave her a wry look. 'It will be months before you're back to normal, but does it really matter? It took nine months to grow her, so you should allow yourself at least nine months to recover. That's my view.'

Anna gently stroked her daughter's face with her little finger. 'She was totally worth it, anyway. Who cares about the pain or the baby fat? Look at her.'

They all peered at the sleeping baby. She boasted a mop of fine hair, as dark as Anna's, and her eyelashes swept her chubby cheeks as she slept, one little fist clenched against her rosebud mouth.

'She's so gorgeous,' Izzy murmured. 'I'm so proud of you, Anna.'

Anna smiled warmly at her. 'Thanks, Izz. I'm pretty proud of myself to be honest.'

'Yes,' Holly said, her eyes wide, 'but did it *hurt*?'

Anna gritted her teeth. 'Let's just say, it wasn't comfortable, but it doesn't seem to matter now. Nothing really matters now that she's here and she's healthy.'

Connor, Ash and Xander returned, carrying drinks and biscuits. Somehow, they all managed to squash onto sofas or in chairs, though it was a tight squeeze.

Izzy glanced around the room, noting the array of congratulations cards that had already arrived for the new parents. There were dozens of them. News had spread fast around the village, and Maudie's shop had been inundated with customers, hurrying to buy cards. Needless to say, there were several duplicates.

Ash and Izzy had gone into Helmston early that morning to do Izzy's Christmas grocery shop, and while they were there they'd bought a card, a pink foil balloon, flowers for Anna and several pretty dresses for the new arrival.

'And not in newborn size,' Izzy had assured Anna. 'I reckon she'll be too big for those babygrows you got her in a matter of days. Ooh,' she'd gently pinched the baby's cheek, 'she's so beautiful. I can't wait to cuddle her.'

'Go ahead,' Anna had said, laughing, and Izzy had held the baby to her, breathing in that special smell that only new babies have. She'd looked across at Ash and they'd smiled at each other, knowing that it was all okay. They loved other people's children, loved being part of their lives. And that was all they needed.

The best part of it was, their friends seemed to have accepted it and understood it without any protests. When Izzy had hesitantly informed them all that she and Ash were together, and explained the story behind their break-up and reconciliation, there had been no cries of, 'But Ash would make such a good father!' which was what she'd feared. Instead there had been cries of delight and lots of hugs. Ash was welcomed into the fold as Xander and Riley had been before them. Speaking of which . . .

'Where are Nell and Riley?' Holly voiced the question that Izzy had only just formed in her mind. 'I thought they'd be the first to be here.'

'So did I,' Izzy said, catching Anna's eye.

Anna smiled. 'They should be here very soon, don't worry.' She glanced at her watch. 'Any moment now, I reckon.'

It was, however, two cups of tea later when the door opened, and Nell and Riley burst in, looking flushed and happy and carrying yet another pink balloon and a large teddy bear with a pink bow.

'Congratulations!' Riley shook Connor's hand enthusiastically as Nell hugged Anna. 'Let's have a look at the wee girl.' He leaned over and gazed at the baby in awe. 'She's beautiful,' he assured the proud parents. 'I can only think she has more of Anna in her than you, Connor,' he added, nudging his colleague with a laugh.

'What are you going to call her?' Nell asked. 'Is it still Eloise after your mum?'

All eyes turned to Anna. She glanced

over at Connor and he smiled back. 'It is,' she confirmed. 'Eloise Isobel Blake. Eloise after her grandmother, and — ' she hesitated, 'and Isobel after her godmother.' She looked directly at Izzy. 'If that's all right with you?'

Izzy's mouth fell open. 'Me? Godmother?' Her face heated up with shame as she thought about all the awful assumptions she'd made about Anna. 'Are you sure?' She glanced across at Nell, worried she would be put out that she hadn't been chosen, but Nell was beaming up at Riley and he had his arms wrapped around her and neither seemed in the slightest bit surprised or upset.

'Who else would I ask?' Anna said softly. 'You're my best friend, Izz. Of course I want you to be her godmother.'

Ash took Izzy's hand as her eyes filled with tears. 'I'd love it. Thank you so much, both of you. I don't know what to say.'

'You said yes,' Connor said comfortably, 'and I think that's all you need to say, isn't it?'

'What a day this has turned out to be,' Holly said, shaking her head. 'A new baby, Ash and Izzy together, and tomorrow is Christmas Eve. I guess you won't be going to the carol service then, Anna?'

Anna laughed. 'I don't think so, no. But Dottie wants to go and she's going to take Gracie.'

'How is Gracie taking the new arrival?' Ash asked. 'Is she okay?'

Izzy felt a warm glow inside her. Trust Ash to think of Gracie and worry about her. He was so wonderful.

'To be honest,' Connor said, 'she's barely glanced at her. We introduced them, of course, and Gracie sort of looked at her and asked a few questions, then she went off and hasn't really bothered since.' He sighed. 'Right now, she's more interested in choosing a dog than in her new sister.'

Anna gave him a sympathetic look. 'But we knew that might happen, didn't we? Give her time, Connor.'

He nodded, and Xander cleared his

throat. 'Well,' he said, 'there's no champagne in the house which, frankly, is a disgrace, but let's raise our mugs of tea instead. A toast — to our new arrival, Miss Eloise Isobel Blake.'

'Eloise Isobel Blake,' everyone toasted.

'And to Ash and Izzy,' Rachel added. 'Because if ever a couple belonged together, it's these two, and I'm so glad you both realised it at last.'

'To Ash and Izzy,' everyone agreed, raising their mugs once again.

Izzy was just about to take a sip of tea when Anna piped up, 'And one more toast, I think, don't you?' She looked at Nell and Riley. 'Don't you have something you'd like to share?'

Nell and Riley looked at each other and smiled. 'Aye, we do,' Riley said. 'Two things, in fact.' He hugged Nell to him. 'This morning, Nell and I were away to the registry office in Whitby, and I'm happy to say she's made an honest man of me at last.'

There was a stunned silence, then lots of squeals followed by several shushes as they remembered the sleeping baby on Anna's lap.

'You're married!' Holly threw her arms around the happy couple. 'I can't believe it! How come you didn't tell us?'

'Och, you know how we feel about weddings.' Riley tutted. 'It's our day, and neither of us would have wanted it any other way.'

'I'm so happy for you both,' Izzy said. She glanced over at Anna. 'I'm guessing you knew?'

Anna nodded.

'Don't blame Anna,' Nell said hastily. 'I asked her to say nothing. She knew because we'd asked her and Connor to be our witnesses. Of course, that plan went awry at the last moment, but we always knew it was a risk. Anyway, we got Chloe and her husband to stand in at the last moment. We nipped to the registry office then had lunch in a restaurant and that was it. It was all we wanted and we're very happy.'

'Very happy,' Riley confirmed. He

beamed round at them all. 'Nell and I are delighted to announce that there'll be another wee arrival in June.'

'You're kidding!' Holly was clearly stunned. 'I don't believe it. How come I never knew about any of this?'

'Because you're too loved up with Jonathan to take any notice,' Rachel told her. 'If you hadn't been, you might have noticed the clues.' She eyed Izzy steadily. 'Like Nell's sudden interest in pram shopping and wanting to accompany Anna on her hospital appointments.'

Izzy's cheeks burned. So that was why! It wasn't Anna pushing for Nell's company at all, it was Nell who wanted to find out more about what was in store for her.

'I'm sorry we couldn't tell you all,' Nell said. 'Connor, Anna and Rachel knew because of the pregnancy test and ante-natal records, but I wanted to keep it quiet from everyone else because — well, you know, things can go wrong. I wanted to get the scan out of the way first, and we had that on Tuesday.

Everything was fine, so we feel happy to share our news with you at last.'

Which was why Nell had been missing from Spill the Beans on one of their busiest days. Izzy had seriously misjudged her. Assumptions. That was her problem. She'd made assumptions all along: about Anna's feelings towards her after revealing she didn't want children; about how Ash would react when she confessed the truth to him; and about Nell's motives for hanging around Anna so much. She'd got everything so wrong, and she was very lucky that no one seemed to be harbouring a grudge.

There was a knock on the door and Connor rolled his eyes. 'Don't think we're going to fit anyone else in here.'

He hurried into the hallway, returning a few minutes later with a woman that Izzy didn't recognise. She looked pretty harassed, her shoulder-length tawny hair rather wind-blown, her cheeks red from the cold, her coat damp from the snow. She looked around at everyone, seeming — unsurprisingly — taken aback at such a large crowd.

'Golly,' she said cheerfully, 'I didn't expect an audience. Just came to drop you a Christmas card off on my way home. We moved in yesterday,' she added, addressing Connor. 'It's a bit of a stupid time to move, with Christmas practically here, but we figured why not? It's chaos at home but it all adds to the fun.'

At several blank faces, Connor pulled himself together. 'Sorry, sorry. Everyone, this is Dr Abbie Sawdon. She's our new GP and she'll be starting in the New Year. Abbie, these are our friends, Izzy, Ash, Rachel, Xander, and Holly. Rachel's our nurse so you'll be seeing quite a bit of her. Anna, Nell and Riley you already know, of course.'

'And this,' added Anna, 'is our new baby daughter, Eloise Isobel.'

'Oh, isn't she gorgeous! When did she arrive?' Abbie leaned over and smiled at the baby.

'Early Thursday morning,' Connor said. 'What a night that was! Nine pounds three ounces,' he added proudly.

Abbie straightened and puffed out her cheeks. 'Good grief. Mind you, I'm not surprised. When I last saw you, Anna, I thought you were about to burst.'

Izzy grinned. She had a feeling she was going to like Abbie.

'Well, I won't stay. Got a car full of kids and dogs outside and they're all demanding food. Merry Christmas, everyone!'

They all chorused merry Christmas back at her and, as she hurried out of the room followed by Connor, there was a general murmuring of agreement that she was very likeable and would fit right in with the rest of them.

Eloise chose that moment to wake up, and the air was filled with an ear-splitting baby's cry.

Funnily enough, everyone decided that it was time they left the little family in peace. Rachel called for Sam and there followed ten minutes of finding coats, scarves and boots, and a general melee as people hugged and said their goodbyes. Anna handed Eloise to Connor, and he rocked her gently in his arms as he and Anna stood, side-by-side on the doorstep, waving them all off to their respective homes.

'Will you be at the Christmas carol concert tomorrow?' Nell asked, as they crowded round the front gate after Anna had closed the door. She and Riley were about to head right to The Ducklings. Rachel, Xander and Sam were going back to Folly Farm in the car, while Izzy and Ash were going left to Rose Cottage.

Izzy glanced at Ash. 'I'll be going. Is that okay with you?'

'I'd love to,' he assured her.

'We'll see you there,' Xander promised.

After exchanging further hugs, they each headed home. Izzy hooked her arm through Ash's as they crunched through the snow.

'I never asked you,' she said, as they

reached the front door of Rose Cottage and she turned to face him. 'What are your plans for Christmas Day?'

Ash tilted his head to one side, pretending to think about it. 'Hmm. Tricky. So many options . . . '

Izzy shrugged. 'It's just that, I have an invitation to join Mum and Dad in Spain and I've already told them I'd go.'

Ash's face dropped. 'Seriously?'

'Seriously,' she admitted. 'I thought you and I were through, and I didn't want to be sitting here alone on Christmas Day so . . . '

He bit his lip, considering. 'I guess if they're expecting you . . . I'll miss you. Will you be gone long?'

She laughed and threw her arms around his neck. 'You're so easy! As if I'd leave you here alone!'

The relief on his face was palpable. 'So, you were having me on?'

'Not entirely,' she confessed. 'They did ask me, and I did say yes, but I told them last night about us and that I would be staying here, spending a cosy Christmas with the love of my life in Rose Cottage. Is that okay?'

'More than okay.' He pulled her to him. 'Love of your life, eh?'

'Might be,' she said. 'Oh, and before I forget, they suggested I fly out for New Year's Day instead. And they extended the invitation to you, if you'd like to meet them?'

Ash kissed the tip of her nose. 'I think I should, because I have a feeling they're going to be a part of my life from now on. What do you think?'

'I think you're right,' she said. 'And on that note — ' She rummaged in her coat pocket and pulled out a sprig of mistletoe. 'Time for my Christmas kiss.'

'Where did you get that?' he said, laughing.

'Grabbed it from your flat,' she admitted. 'The way you treat your decorations, I didn't trust you with its care. I'm giving it a home at Rose Cottage for the holidays.' She gazed up at him, her expression hopeful. 'I was thinking, maybe you'd like to spend Christmas here, too. Just to keep an eye on it.'

'If I stay for Christmas,' he said, 'I may never want to leave.'

'That suits me fine,' she murmured. 'Now about that kiss?'

Mistletoe was awfully useful as Christmas decorations went, she mused, but, of course, Christmas wouldn't last forever, and she wouldn't always have a sprig of mistletoe to hand.

Izzy wasn't worried, though. She had a warm and wonderful feeling that she and Ash would always manage perfectly well without it.

Not that she liked to make assumptions . . .